THE OLD UNIVERSE

STORY BY
ERIC MARTINEZ AND ARMANI SALADO
WRITTEN BY
ARMANI SALADO

The Old Universe was created by
Forbidden Origins LLC

No part of this publication may be reproduced in whole or in part, or stored in retrieval system, or transmitted in any form or by any means, electronic, mechanical, photocopying, recording or otherwise, without written permission of the publisher. For information regarding permission, email Forbidden Origins at contact@forbiddenorigins.com

The Old Universe ISBN 9780578399072
copyright © 2022 by Forbidden Origins LLC

Printed in the U.S.A.

CONTENTS

PROLOGUE I

Chapter 1: Halvodon 1
Chapter 2: A Time of Life When Mountains Had Breath........... 22
Chapter 3: Dangerous Winds Ahead 43
Chapter 4: The Rider of Rashalon 63
Chapter 5: Our Actions Define Us.. 83
Chapter 6: New Worlds 102
Chapter 7: The Division... 117
Chapter 8: We Are With You 133
Chapter 9: Lines Are Drawn 158
Chapter 10: War in the Universe 178
Chapter 11: The Allegiance 194
Chapter 12: The First Year 216

Glossary 246

THE OLD UNIVERSE

PROLOGUE

In the beginning, there was nothing. The existence of life, matter, and all things the eye could see were not yet made viable, until the spears.

As the vast emptiness of the void continued, matter for the first time began to take shape in the form of the ideals of time and space.

Formulated through an energy unknown, time and space morphed out of the void into existing substances. A swift change fluttered throughout the void.

Alive, touchable, and with what seemed like minds of their own, time and space were there as the first beings in the vast emptiness of the void, until the spears.

Floating through the void as lost passengers in a sea of endless white emptiness, time and space took control of their newfound existence and capitalized off their unguided journey.

Intrigued by one another, time and space grew to understand that they were created to balance each other out.

Cycles went by, and the auras of time and space transformed into what looked like orbs of unimaginable power and infinite knowledge.

Time drowned out the blankness of the void with its almost blinding luminosity of curiosity and sense of direction, while space gave off a darker sense of authority and control.

The now more mature orbs of time and space were ready to question what they could do. So, they took what they knew a step further beyond their existence by creating the spears.

Zooming through the void, the orbs of time and space began to shed their circular forms. Out of their destruction came the forging of two spears that now embodied the luminosity and authority of time and space.

The two new spears of time and space radiated power beyond belief. Sleek in their newfound mantles, the spears were massive. They each shared similar characteristics, both having immense blades at the tip. The void was too small for the spears, so expansion was needed.

The spears gradually inched toward each other. Throughout the void, the essence of silence began to shatter. The nothingness of the void quaked and rippled as the spears reached each other.

The eerie calmness of nothing shifted into a whirlwind of uncertainty as the spears grew closer and closer together. As their collision was imminent, the era of the void was at its end.

The spears of time and space clashed, releasing life, matter, and infinite existence out of themselves and into the void, consuming the void with a new sea of black and stars. The universe was now born.

With the fresh universe scourging with uncontrollable amounts of energy, the spears' magnetic connection to one another was now even stronger.

Omniscient in their existence and proud of their achievement, the spears realized that their collision sparked a new chapter. But with their clash, they understood that destruction could follow if they were to ever touch again. Fighting the urge to collide once more, the spears devised a plan to have holders ensure the survival of their creation, the universe.

The spears of time and space consumed the surrounding stars, shattering the burning balls of fire into trillions of atoms. The spears transformed and forged the particles, molding them together. Eventually they each spawned an entity that would be the guardian, or bearer, of each spear.

Created from within the spears, two life-forms emerged. Energy slithered out into the universe, revealing legs, thighs, torsos, arms, chests, and heads. From the smelted down stars life was born.

Undeveloped and glossed with scattering animations of barely structured bodies, the two forms fluttered in the midst of the young universe. They were translucent in the vast darkness of the universe. Uncontrollable amounts of energy were scourged from their unfinished skins. Protected by the spears, the hovering and developing anatomies slept in a state of growth.

As years, centuries, and cycles went by, the anatomies spawned by the spears were ready to emerge from their forming stage.

Physically developed, and somewhat aware of their existence, the spawns of time and space took hold of their individual spears for the first time.

Fully capable now of moving, living, and thinking on their own, the spears of time and space filtered all of their power into their holders. Conscious, the holders of the spears now knew that the spears were capable of life and destruction, and that the survival of the universe was now in their hands.

The holder of the Spear of Time was named Zaman, while the Spear of Space named its holder Nox. Zaman and Nox understood that if the spears were to ever clash again, the universe that was now their home would be destroyed.

Young in their existence and as holders of the spears, Zaman and Nox went their separate ways, each exploring the universe on their own.

THE OLD UNIVERSE

As Zaman traveled the universe in an attempt to understand time and be a keeper of its history of all things, Nox felt the power of the Spear of Space push him to a more evolving destiny.

As cycles went by of Nox floating alone throughout the universe, he used the spear to create a planet.

New at this attempt, Nox's planet was misshapen, with a brutal landscape. He then attempted to create a home for himself, which was later named The Black Palace.

The Black Palace was an enormous fortress that was erected out of his home planet's atmosphere and into space, giving him a bird's-eye view of the entire universe.

Pleased with this, Nox then sent out a blast of power from the Spear of Space into the universe. A blast that started a ripple effect of planets being formed.

As time went by, Nox wanted his new planets to have inhabitants like him, and once again used the Spear of Space to create people.

His creations were spread all over each planet and were given the ability to do, act, and believe in whatever they wanted. Nox was filled with pleasure and excitement about being a beacon of new life in the universe and continued this blueprint throughout all the galaxies.

He spent time on each planet, interacting with his creations and watched them each flourish in their own ways. As years went by, Nox was now seen as a God, a bringer of life. He then changed his name to The All Father.

The All Father used so much spear energy to create life in the universe that it took a toll on his body. A toll that put him into a deep sleep for more than eight cycles.

When he finally awoke from what would later be called The Long Sleep, he never thought the universe would be thriving with trillions of souls he considered his children.

Massive in height, and towering over anyone in his presence, The All Father loomed over the universe from the shadows of his fortress, alone and in a state of disarray.

His blank white eyes told a story of ambition and uncertainty. The vast universe and all its wonders were laid out in front of his dark blue skin, but his mind couldn't grasp the entirety of it all without feeling empty inside.

In the early years, he was captivated and in awe of the inhabitants of the worlds, intrigued by their smaller physiques, short life expectancies, and remarkable sense of love and nurturing.

The knowledge of how they formed their own civilizations, thoughts, codes of honor, systems of governing, and warfare made him admire the free people of the universe.

Seeing babies born naturally and grow into formidable men and women led him to want to have a child. After being alone in the universe as the creator of all, The All Father wanted to truly father and raise a child he could call his own.

Faded from distant memory, The All Father began to travel the planets in disguise. The inhabitants of each world were either welcoming or cold to his arrival, none knowing he was the creator of all they knew.

As time went on, The All Father grew tired of trying to find the love he ached for. His emptiness of never being able to have what his creations had began to eat at him, until he came across a being of beauty more enchanting than the brightest supernova.

"Hello," The All Father said to her softly, his voice almost trembling the trees.

Her hair was black as night, her skin fair and glowing. The All Father had been to every planet in the universe, to every solar system, to every gaping hole known to him, but nothing ever made him feel what he felt seeing this creation for the first time.

She looked up at him, her green gaze forcing its way into The All Father's veins, making them pulsate like never before. He knew she was the one immediately.

Many are unsure if this was destiny, the work of the spears or just pure natural love at first sight. But whatever it was, it led to The All Father wanting more.

"What is your name?" he asked her.

"Helena," she replied.

She looked deeply at him, unafraid of who this man was or what his intentions were. She answered in a way that almost seemed like she knew he was there for her.

The All Father and Helena lusted over each other for weeks, exploring her world and falling for each other more and more each day.

Helena's home planet was Yres, a blue world of water people and fishermen. Their way of life was peaceful compared to the other worlds The All Father had seen, and very different from the mindset The All Father had himself.

The All Father was amazed at how humble Helena's people were and was hesitant to reveal himself to her. He wasn't afraid to show her his true appearance, but he was nervous she would treat him differently if she knew he was the Father of the universe.

As they spent more time together, The All Father felt comfortable enough to reveal his true self to her. He took her to a grand waterfall on Yres and pointed up to the stars.

"What do you know of the universe, Helena?"

Helena was staring at the stars and answered him. "I know it's a giant sea of wonders. I like to think of it as a canvas of life and unexpected surprises," she said, turning her head to The All Father and touching his face.

The All Father looked into her eyes and felt ready to finally tell her who he was. He stood up and extended his hand to the sky. The clouds began to split and out of the atmosphere came zooming down the Spear of Space.

As the spear reached his hand, The All Father's appearance shattered and his true form was revealed. He stood over Helena with his piercing white eyes and dark blue skin. His bare chest was slightly covered by his black drapes and thick cloak.

The Spear of Space was twice Helena's size. He expected resistance or shock but instead was met with Helena smiling at him, almost as if she already knew who he really was.

The All Father had found love, and the emptiness he felt before was now filled with showing Helena the universe. He gave her his hand, big enough to fit both of hers in it, and flew her across the stars.

He showed her Pugart, the world of tribal desert beings. They landed in the Faoder Sector, where some of the first beings had created massive statues of The All Father.

Miles away, The All Father showed Helena Kaasiar, a green planet with valleys as far as the eye could see. He flew her to Nyla, a massive, harsh world full of caverns and mountain ranges.

He showed her the farthest, most deserted lands of the universe, excited in his chance to share it all with her.

On the highest mountain of Nyla, The All Father and Helena sat looking at the moons.

"All this will be yours, my love. The planets, the stars, the universe will be under our command, and in time, the command of our child."

The All Father was drunk with thoughts of the future and his plan to once again show the universe that he was the creator, and that Helena would give his subjects a child to lead them as well.

Throughout their travels, The All Father had told Helena everything about the universe, the spears, Zaman, and his real name. He wanted her to know as much about it all so she could rule the universe as mightily as he dreamed she would.

Helena was aware of the time The All Father had spent alone, how he felt about his creations forgetting him, and how he wanted a family of his own. She listened to his plans to conquer it all under one planetary kingdom and saw how determined he was to claim it all once more.

"Nox. All of this is yours—you gave the universe a life it's never known. The people of these worlds owe you their gratitude, but you gave them free will to live, rule, and be as they are without you hovering over them. When we have a child, it will be ours. Yours. And the universe will go on without having to know about us, our family, and what you gave them."

The All Father's intentions to rule over the universe as one kingdom were shattered by Helena's words. He wanted the universe to once again bow to his feet as the benevolent Father that had given them everything, but he wanted Helena and his own child more.

He left his idea of conquering the universe in Nyla and swore to Helena that she and their child would be his world and only priority.

After showing Helena all the corners of the universe, The All Father finally took her to The Black Palace. His keepers of the Palace were intrigued by Helena, a mortal being from another world who was now the first outside resident in The All Father's home.

Within the first year of Helena living in The Black Palace, she bore The All Father a son named Corrin. Half mortal, half eternal, The All Father now had a child truly of his own. Corrin had his mother's hair, black as night. He shared both his parents' eyes, one white as snow and the other greener than the valleys of Kaasiar.

But tragedy struck The Black Palace the day Corrin was born. Helena was in labor for days and died during childbirth. Her mortal body gave out before she was able to hold her son, but she was able to utter what she wanted him to be named before her soul passed on.

The All Father was destroyed by the news. He stumbled in trying to use the Spear of Space to revive Helena's body, but it didn't work. The Spear of Space is able to give life but not sustain it. It can create but cannot reanimate that which has expired.

"This cannot be! This was not supposed to happen!" The All Father yelled.

He held Helena's lifeless body for days before allowing The Black Palace's wards to give her a burial.

He grieved for months in solitude. During this time, he considered destroying The Black Palace with everyone inside, even his newborn son. For the first time in his existence, The All Father felt emotions he never knew of. His demeanor as the all-powerful being who wields the Spear of Space was questioned.

During his time of solitude, he tried manifesting knowledge of these emotions from the Spear, but it didn't help him understand. He was for the first time feeling sadness, loss, and mortality itself. He couldn't fathom the feeling of devoting oneself to someone and then having that someone taken away so quickly. He vowed to never feel like that again.

His sadness eventually turned to bitterness, and his vision of the universe was clear. The All Father stayed in solitude contemplating his next move before enacting his plan and giving his newborn son his love and guidance.

Hovering over The Black Palace with Corrin resting in his hands, The All Father cemented his son's destiny.

"My son, you will live and grow to know what's yours," he said to baby Corrin before revealing himself to the universe once again.

The All Father walked heavily, but determined, to the top of The Black Palace to once again sit on his throne. A throne that gazes upon the universe. As he sat down, he spoke with authority that was heard throughout the entire universe.

"Creations amongst the stars, this is your Father speaking. I have been away from you, watching you from afar. I have returned now as your leader, your God, and your reason to exist. Disband your governments. Forget your laws. My word is now the authority of all the lands, by my command. The Black Palace is the capital of all now. My children, my beautiful creations, your Father is here!"

CHAPTER 1

HALVODON

When his tenth year came, emissaries from across the universe came to The Black Palace to pay tribute to The All Father and his son, Corrin.

Corrin was to rule one day and it was out of either respect, or fear, that the planets under The All Father's control came to bear witness and show respect to their future leader.

Corrin was a curious young boy, open-minded to what he saw and learned, and welcoming of all types of beings. Unlike The All Father, his mother's acceptance of others was prominent with him, and it was something he kept for years to come. Although his tenth year marked a transition of a boy living in The Black Palace to becoming a future ruler, the thought of leaving home to study the known planets never scared Corrin.

With his chin-length hair darker than the blackest hole and thicker than the toughest hide of the largest ice creatures on Catovaz, Corrin was ready to see all that would one day be his.

The All Father wanted Corrin to be trained in the many arts of combat, fluent in multiple languages, and well-read with the vast amounts of literature across the planetary kingdom.

Corrin was becoming aware of the civilizations under his Father's control and during his years abroad, he made many friends away from The Black Palace and formed lifelong relationships.

During his years abroad, he even spent time in the Sanctuary of Time with Zaman, the keeper of all history and holder of the Spear of Time.

"C'mon, Zaman, let me just swing it around. I'm trained to hold weapons bigger and heavier than this," Corrin exclaimed to Zaman, trying to grab the Spear of Time from its resting pedestal.

By this time, Corrin was fifteen years old. His thick black hair was long, and his young body was in top-tier shape from training across the universe. The boyish looks he left home with were starting to turn into those of a young man.

"Only a little boy, still consumed by trivial imagination of what is and what is not, would consider the Spears of Time and Space to be weapons," Zaman said while recording a new event in the Book of Time.

Zaman's white eyes resembled those of The All Father's. His light blue skin and white hair glowed under the stars as he peered into his sanctuary.

"Well, my Father says that the spears are the strongest things in the universe and that one would be a fool not to use them to their full potential," Corrin said, practicing a new martial arts form taught to him from his previous destination.

Zaman, still recording something into the Book of Time, replied, "Your Father wishes to use the Spear of Space as a tool of power, but it's up to you to decide how you wish to manifest your own destiny."

Corrin, stopping in the middle of his form, took a minute to digest Zaman's words, words that would mean everything in the years to come.

"What are you even writing in that book?" he asked Zaman.

"Come, take a look," Zaman said, finishing the last sentence.

Corrin walked over to the massive book, with millions of pages filled with dates, names, events, and cycles.

He focused his eyes on what Zaman was writing.

"Is that from today?" he asked, touching the book and feeling a sense of all history rush through his body.

"Yes it is. All moments throughout time are precious and meaningful. Understanding it all is a key to the future," Zaman said, placing his hand on Corrin's shoulder.

Intrigued by it all, Corrin tried to flip to the next page, but Zaman stopped him quickly, informing him, "What lies ahead of time is not for us to know, Corrin. The future is set, and tampering with the ripple of time is detrimental to what is to come, and what is to happen."

Corrin pondered this thought, taking in Zaman's words.

"Have you ever looked ahead?"

"No," Zaman said, walking to his chambers. "I record time as it happens, and what happens is meant to be as time delivers it."

Corrin left Zaman as a curious, stubborn teenager with much to learn, not knowing that the next time they would meet would be when Corrin was an adult during the direst time.

Corrin continued his travels across the universe, still gathering knowledge of its vast entirety and becoming more and more in tune with how the people lived, and how they viewed his Father's rule.

Some planets worshipped The All Father and treated Corrin as a God upon his arrival, while others had different sentiments.

Corrin's curiosity as a teenage boy almost always led him to stray away from his traveling guard on each planet they visited, getting him into all sorts of trouble and problems, especially on Halvodon.

Halvodon wasn't on Corrin's itinerary of planets to travel to and study on, but the planet was in a book he "borrowed" from Zaman's sanctuary.

Wondering why Halvodon wasn't on his list, he decided to go there to see the planet and its people. He told himself that if his Father wished for him to rule the entire universe one day, then he should visit the entire universe, even planets not on his list.

What Corrin didn't know was that Halvodon was a planet his Father had almost destroyed during the building of the empire.

The inhabitants of Halvodon were hesitant to fall in line under The All Father's decree of a unified planetary kingdom, and so they fought against the idea with force while Corrin was an infant.

The Halvodis managed to fight off The All Father's armies but were no match when The All Father decided to fight them himself.

"Syeron, we're going to make a stop before our next destination."

"Where to?" asked Syeron, Corrin's navigator and trusted advisor.

Syeron had been Corrin's navigator throughout his entire travels across the universe. He was from Fargulk, a planet close to The Black Palace, and had been part of the first campaigns to build The All Father's empire.

His bald head always made Corrin laugh, getting him on Syeron's bad side throughout most of their travels.

The Fargulkians were large beings. Some called them giants, but the people of Fargulk took that comment as an insult. Their brute size, massive hands, and muscular structures were the reason The All Father enlisted them to be the first members of his army, and why The All Father trusted Syeron to be Corrin's traveling companion.

"This better not be one of your little tricks again. I'm not getting you out of another fight with a warlord," Syeron ranted. "Remember that girl on Taelvum?! Her father wanted your head!"

Corrin laughed, remembering it as if it were yesterday.

"Where is it you want to go this time?!" Syeron asked in a more serious tone.

Corrin leaned in.

"Have you heard of Halvodon?"

Syeron abruptly stopped the ship and turned over to Corrin, glaring into his eyes.

"Where did you hear that name?" Syeron demanded, grabbing Corrin's things and ransacking through them.

The book Corrin had borrowed from Zaman's sanctuary fell to the floor and Syeron picked it up.

THE OLD UNIVERSE 7

"You stole this from the Time Keeper, didn't you?!" Syeron exclaimed, throwing the book across the ship.

"The All Father will have my head if I take you to Halvodon," Syeron said to himself, pacing back and forth.

During Syeron's outburst, Corrin watched the whole time in amusement. He was somewhat thrilled at seeing Syeron all worked up.

"Syeron," Corrin said laughing, "calm down. I just want to do a flyover of the planet and record what I see."

Corrin stood up and walked over to pick up the book he had taken from Zaman's chambers.

"You don't know Halvodon, or what the people there are capable of, Corrin!" Syeron exclaimed, his tone more nervous and chilling than ever.

Corrin picked up the book from the ground, frustrated.

"How am I expected to rule the universe one day if I'm not familiar with *all* that is *supposed* to be mine?!"

Syeron sat down in his seat, listening to young Corrin.

"Everything out there amongst the stars is under The Black Place now, whether those inhabitants like it or not. And if I want to be half the ruler my Father is, I think I should start by understanding every civilization and what their wants and needs are."

Corrin placed his hand on the ship's window and looked out into the stars. He continued speaking, "I want them to love and respect me without fear or intimidation. I want them to know I am one of them."

Syeron stood up and walked to Corrin, sighing. "You're young, but wiser than the oldest beings in all the galaxies. Not everyone will want to understand and learn from each other, but a great leader can unite the worlds under a banner of peace." Syeron walked back to the wheel of the ship and set course to Halvodon.

"Only a flyover. But I warn you, Corrin, the Halvodis have painful memories of the last time someone from The Black Palace came into their atmosphere. They do not share your sentiment of peace."

Corrin sat back down in his seat and strapped in.

"That will change soon," Corrin said, gripping his seat as Syeron took off.

As hours on the ship went by, Corrin began to get bored of sitting and standing. The ship they were on was used for large troop movement, but when Corrin began his travels, The All Father decommissioned it to be solely used for Corrin. Its large interior was usually filled with Black Palace soldiers, medics, intelligence officers, and even prisoners. But with just Corrin and

Syeron on board, the feeling of being alone was strongly felt throughout its empty corridors.

"Syeron, how much longer? Why don't we just dock the ship at one of the ports and glide there?"

When the Itarians discovered space travel during The Long Sleep, they scoured the galaxies on their cosmic dragons, bringing technology and advancement to the worlds. Spacecrafts were invented for Itarian troop movement, and later used for travel amongst the worlds. But when The All Father used the spear to create life in the universe, the power of the spear was so full of pure energy that it enabled certain individuals to fly, and even breathe in space, making travel for those with lots of spear energy inside them faster and more efficient.

"Well, for one, I can't breathe in space like you, Corrin. And two, Halvodon is far away. On the way are outlaw ships and raid riders. It's too dangerous to fly there without an armed ship, especially for someone like you."

Corrin slumped back into his seat and crossed his arms, stubbornly thinking that he could easily take on any outlaw or raid rider.

As more hours passed, Corrin began reading more on the Halvodis from the book he took from Zaman's library. The book told tales of the Halvodis, how beautiful and rich of life their planet was, and how the Halvodis lived. It had depictions of large waterfalls with fields of green with animals of all sorts grazing. The book told how magnificent and advanced the Halvodis were as well.

They were a race of civilized beings, gathering resources not only for individual prosperity but for their neighbor as well. The book explained how they didn't believe in war, and instead believed in a complete harmony of fellowship and community.

"We are approaching Halvodon," Syeron said, taking a deep breath without letting Corrin see.

Halvodon sat lonely in deep space, accompanied by three moons and a nearby ring of asteroids. Two suns in this galaxy shone on the planet, bringing Corrin joy to see the world he had read about in daylight.

As Syeron brought the ship into Halvodon's atmosphere, Corrin jumped to the window, excited to see the large waterfalls, green fields, and grazing animals Zaman's book depicted.

But as the ship descended under the clouds and the surface of the planet became more visible to Corrin, what he saw shocked him. The Halvodon he read about in his borrowed book was not the Halvodon he was looking at with his eyes.

What he saw made him, for the first time in his young life, question what was true and what was not.

As Syeron got closer to the surface of Halvodon and flew across the land, Corrin glared at the wasteland he was witnessing.

The green fields of roaming animals were now burnt miles of rock and ash. Carcasses of animals were spread out as far as the eye could see.

As Syeron took the ship over a bare mountain range, the rest of the planet was just as barren. The hills where the waterfalls must have once rushed down to the valley were now dried up and deserted of any sort of life.

Corrin felt his stomach churn and his skin began to crawl. He was in utter dismay at how destroyed Halvodon was.

"Syeron," Corrin said quietly. "What happened here?"

Corrin continued to stare out into the dead landscapes. Deep down he already knew the answer to his question, but he didn't want to let his heart and mind address the truth.

Syeron kept his eyes focused on the air, not answering him. Corrin looked at Syeron and couldn't tell if the emptiness he saw in his eyes was from fear of being in Halvodi territory or if he was hiding something from him.

He walked over to the passenger seat next to Syeron and sat down, trying to get a better look at Syeron's eyes.

"You've been here before, haven't you?" Corrin asked.

"You know what happened to this place. Tell me why this planet looks different from my book!" Corrin demanded.

His fear of what the truth might be turned into anger as Sycron began to explain.

"You were only a few months old when this happened," Sycron stated, his voice almost trembling at the thought of retelling a painful memory.

"None of us knew this would happen. It was unexpected. Your fathe—" As Sycron tried to finish his sentence, the ship carrying them was drastically hit by something that caused the ship to go into a free fall.

"Strap in now! We've been hit!" Sycron yelled, frantically trying to regain control of the ship.

Corrin ran to his seat and buckled himself in, looking out the window with wide eyes as one of the ship's wings was up in a blaze. The ship was falling fast to the surface of Halvodon, losing power and function the closer it got to the ground.

"What happened?!" Corrin yelled from his seat.

Sycron desperately unbuckled his seat belt and rushed back to Corrin.

"We've taken damage and are crashing down fast."

About three times the size of young Corrin, Sycron ripped off Corrin's seat belt and wrapped him in a cocoon in his arms.

"What are you doing?!" yelled Corrin.

"Saving your life," Syeron said as the ship reached the ground.

Both of them closed their eyes and braced for impact as the ship smashed into the dirt. The engine exploded on impact, causing the back portion of the ship to completely rip off. Glass shattered in the ship, piercing Syeron's back and arms. Corrin screamed as the rest of the ship tumbled across the ground.

When the ship finally stopped tumbling and the noise from the destruction stopped, Corrin opened his eyes. He was still wrapped in Syeron's arms, safe from the debris and crash. He pushed himself out of Syeron's arms, falling onto the floor of what remained of the ship.

"Syeron, we're alive. *We're alive!*" Corrin yelled out in excitement.

Corrin waited for Syeron to react in excitement as well but was met with silence.

"Syeron?" Corrin said nervously, pushing on his large arm. Syeron didn't respond.

"*Syeron!*" Corrin yelled, flipping him from his side to face him.

Syeron's eyes were closed. He was losing a dangerous amount of blood. Corrin frantically flipped him onto his stomach, revealing the gashes and shards of glass that had pierced Syeron's back and head.

Corrin drastically began pulling pieces of glass out of Syeron.

"Syeron, please," Corrin begged, as tears ran down his face. "Don't die. I'm sorry for bringing us here. This is all my fault."

Corrin continued pulling out the glass from Syeron's back until he slumped over Syeron's body and sobbed profusely.

"Please wake up. Please wake up."

The crash had completely destroyed the ship, making it unusable. Small pieces of the ship were on fire outside, making Corrin fearful of calling attention to the wreckage. The crash itself had destroyed miles of already decayed trees and plains. As Corrin laid on the ground of what remained of the ship, he passed out over Syeron's body.

The suns of Halvodon were already setting when Corrin woke up to metal clanking and voices. The golden haze from the suns made the barren landscape of Halvodon look beautiful, almost telling a story of what this planet once was.

Corrin looked at Syeron, who still hadn't moved. The voices from outside were getting closer. Corrin silently moved around the ship, looking for anything to defend himself.

He found a large piece of metal broken off from the ship's interior and slid into a corner behind some destroyed materials. As the voices approached the ship, Corrin was able to make out three individuals. They were men.

"It looks abandoned," one of them whispered.

"There hasn't been outside contact in years," another said.

The men speaking began making their way around the ship, inspecting it. Corrin gripped his pseudo-weapon tighter, getting ready to fight if he had to.

As The All Father's son, Corrin had never experienced battle or any sort of physical altercation. Being trained in the arts of combat around the universe had made him a talented warrior for his young age, but his lack of real-world experience still made him terrified of who was outside the ship.

As the individuals approached the head of the craft, Corrin realized they would be able to see Sycron. His mind began to race on what he should do.

"Do you think it's one of His?" asked one of the individuals.

Corrin couldn't see what they looked like but heard them hitting and poking the ship.

"Silence," one of the individuals said, scolding the others. His voice sounded older and harsh.

"The All Father has ears everywhere. Stay alert!" the older individual continued.

Corrin was concerned to hear them speak about his Father. "Ears everywhere?" he said to himself, confused about what they meant by that.

As the men outside continued inspecting the ship, Corrin's focus shifted back to figuring out how he would stop them from seeing Syeron's body. When the men were about to round the corner that would give them a clear view of Syeron, Corrin reacted. He dropped his makeshift weapon and crawled outside.

"Help! Help!" he yelled.

The three men came running back to his side of the ship, saving Syeron from being spotted by them.

As they got to Corrin, two of them helped him up from the ground. They were tall and lanky, with drapes pieced together as clothes. Corrin's lighter complexion was drowned out by their tan, caramel skin.

An older-looking man pushed the other two aside. He had a thick gray beard, with yellow-green eyes glaring at Corrin. He was carrying a large staff with a blade tied to the end. He pointed it at Corrin.

"Who are you? And why are you on Halvodon?!" he demanded.

The other two men actually weren't men at all. They looked about Corrin's age, one maybe older than the other. They were staring wide-eyed at each other.

The older man looked back at them, keeping his weapon pointed at Corrin.

"Boys, draw your knives. We can never be too careful with outsiders," he said, looking Corrin up and down.

The two boys hesitatingly drew knives from what appeared to be wool satchels around their waists. The older man nodded his head, signaling them to circle Corrin, stopping any chance of him trying to make a run for it.

By this time, Corrin had his hands up, not wanting to cause any trouble. He was more concerned about them seeing Syeron and asking more questions.

"I've come here for trade and restocking. My ship needed fuel," Corrin said, lying out of fear.

"Lies. Halvodon hasn't done any sort of trading or refueling in years. You look too young to have been alive when we did," the older-looking boy said, gripping his knife tighter.

"Quiet," the man yelled. He put the blade of his staff up to Corrin's neck and stepped closer to him.

"What are you really doing here?" he said in a low, chilling tone.

"I told you already, my ship needed to be refueled and I lost control as I was trying to land," Corrin said as the younger boy made his way to the inside of the ship.

Corrin knew Syeron was going to be spotted. He was about to use his training and engage with them, but the younger boy let out a scream.

Corrin, the older man, and the older-looking boy turned their heads immediately toward the ship. As the boy stepped back outside from the ship, they saw he was being held by Syeron.

Syeron was holding the boy in a choke hold and had a blade to his neck. The boy was trembling and Syeron could barely stand due to his injuries and blood loss.

"Corrin," he said faintly, "come over here."

Corrin's eyes were wide open. He didn't know what was about to happen.

The old man said quietly to himself, "Corrin?" Then his eyes widened and he yelled angrily, *"Corrin!"*

The older boy also yelled, *"Father, look at his knife. The seal!"*

Syeron's blade's handle had The All Father's insignia on it. A seal in the shape of the orb that had given birth to the spears. A seal on everything that correlates to The All Father, his armies, and his empire.

The older boy grabbed Corrin, but as he did so Corrin flipped him onto his back, making him ache in pain. The older man then hit Corrin in the back with his staff, making him fall to the ground.

"You're the son of The All Father! You've come to scout out if any of us are still alive to finish us off, haven't you?"

Corrin lay on the ground, the older man's blade in his face. Syeron gripped the boy tighter, pressing the blade to the kid's neck.

"Any harm that comes to the son of The All Father will not be in your best interest, Halvodi," Syeron said.

You could hear the pain of his injuries in his voice but also the seriousness of his tone.

The boy Syeron was holding hostage was crying by this point, his tears hitting Syeron's massive forearm like bullets, but not fazing Syeron at all. The older man was breathing heavily. You could tell he wanted to kill Corrin right then and there. He looked at Syeron, then back at Corrin, then back at Syeron.

"I'll signal for an extraction and we will leave your planet. No one has to die today," Syeron said, pressing the knife against the boy's neck even harder, making the boy squirm.

The older boy stood up from the ground, frustrated from Corrin flipping him. The older man pondered Syeron's words, deciding if the young boy's life was worth not killing Corrin.

Corrin, still on the ground, glared at the old man, then looked at Syeron. Syeron was already looking at Corrin, reassuring him with his eyes to stay calm.

The older man then removed his staff from Corrin's face, closed his eyes, and said, "Ancestors forgive me for sacrificing my own blood for vengeance."

Corrin gasped as the older man lifted his staff and went to stab Corrin. Syeron pushed the younger boy to the ground and threw his blade at the older man, piercing his hand and knocking the staff away.

The older man yelled out in pain as Syeron rushed to Corrin. The older boy rushed to his father who was trying to pull Syeron's blade out of his hand.

As Corrin stood, Syeron told him "Run. *Now.*" Corrin stood his ground, holding Syeron from collapsing.

"No. You can barely stand. I'm not leaving you."

The older man pulled the knife out of his hand, blood splattering on his son's face.

"You remember your training? Get back-to-back," Syeron said. His voice was so low and lacked any kind of energy.

The younger boy was still on the ground, fear radiating from his eyes, as he watched his father and older brother circle Corrin and Syeron. The older man picked up his staff, twirling it to get a better grasp. Syeron was much larger than the older man and the older boy, towering over them and Corrin.

"Today you will feel the pain the one you call The All Father has given us," the older man said, charging at Corrin and Syeron.

CHAPTER 2

A TIME OF LIFE WHEN MOUNTAINS HAD BREATH

The older boy charged at them as well. Syeron spun and took on the older man hand-to-hand as Corrin took on the older boy.

Corrin easily evaded the older boy's jabs and swings of the knife. He could tell this kid had no prior training. Syeron and the older man were exchanging jabs. The older man was trying to pierce Syeron with his staff and Syeron was throwing soft punches, losing energy from his wounds every time.

As the four of them were fighting, the younger boy crawled to a satchel his father had dropped. Corrin landed a kick on the older boy's chest, making him drop his knife. As the older boy stumbled back, Corrin picked up his knife.

"Syeron!" Corrin yelled, tossing the knife to him.

Syeron caught the knife, leveling the playing field in his fight with the older man. He jabbed at the older man, cutting his arm. The older man spun and swung his staff sideways, horizontally slicing Syeron's stomach.

Syeron brushed it off and charged at the older man. The older boy was now throwing wild punches at

Corrin, missing every time until one landed, knocking Corrin to the ground.

He straddled Corrin and started pummeling his skull into the ground, making him bleed.

Syeron saw this, making him hip-toss the old man to the ground. He rushed to Corrin with his overpowering size, launching the older boy off him with a stiff arm. As he helped Corrin onto his feet, the younger boy pulled out a horn from his father's satchel and blew it.

The horn wailed loud and echoed off the mountain range. The older boy smirked at the sound, as his father stood up from the ground.

"Go. Now!" Syeron yelled, pointing ahead.

Corrin and Syeron took off, running through the barren wasteland of Halvodon. The young boy blew the horn a few more times. Although he was injured, Syeron ran fast and strong. Corrin, younger and not injured, had trouble keeping up with him, but he was right next to Syeron, in awe at just how strong this Fargulkian was. The older man and his two sons were trailing them.

"We'll lose them over the mountain range," Syeron exclaimed, his voice breathless but still going.

As they ran, they heard more voices all around them. The ground beneath them began to tremble as they heard the loud noises of animals. The sound of multiple horns began to blare in the distance. Corrin looked back as he ran and saw more Halvodis appear over the horizon.

The suns of Halvodon were almost set by now. Silhouettes of hundreds of Halvodis on native riding creatures called Balakars were all Corrin saw. The Balakars were fast for their size. Their bulky, two legged bodies ripped through the Halvodi land. Corrin and Syeron ran faster, terrified of the horde heading their way.

As they ran straight toward the mountain range, more Halvodis appeared on top of the mountain. Some on foot, others riding on Balakars. More appeared to the left of Syeron and on the right of Corrin.

"This way," Syeron yelled, slanting to the left.

Some of the Halvodis began to fly down the mountain range on gliding tech. The horde of Halvodis behind Corrin and Syeron were closing in as were the rest of the riders to both sides of them.

The gliding ones landed in front of them, stopping Corrin and Syeron in their tracks. They were surrounded with nowhere to go. With no backup.

Syeron collapsed onto the dirt, out of breath and aching from his injuries. The Halvodis on top of the mountain range lit arrows on fire and arched back their bows, waiting for Corrin and Syeron to make any sudden movement.

The Halvodis surrounding them were on massive creatures. They resembled the carcasses Corrin saw laid out across the dried-up valleys. Their skin was orange and hairless and they had large purple eyes. All the Halvodis surrounding Corrin and Syeron were dressed like the other three they fought. Armed with more makeshift staffs and swords, they glared down at Corrin.

Syeron was still on the ground gasping for air. One Halvodi, who looked about the same age as the man who had tried to kill Corrin, spoke. His voice was deep and strong, aged with experienced leadership.

"Kill them both. Bring their heads back to Hokdro."

Two Halvodis jumped down from their Balakars and apprehended Corrin as a few others lifted Syeron to his knees. Corrin was shoved down to the ground on his knees. He tried not to show fear. The other three Halvodis from earlier arrived, out of breath. The older man walked up to the Halvodi on the Balakar who gave the order to kill.

"This one looks like a Fargulkian," he said, pointing at Syeron, who was dancing with life and death.

"The boy is Corrin, son of the tyrant," the older man said.

The Halvodi on the Balakar looked down at Corrin, shocked, with his eyes filling with rage. The rest of the Halvodis gasped. Murmurs of disgust and fear rang amongst them.

Corrin looked around at them angrily. He wondered why they hated him and his Father so much. His heart was disrupted at the sound of his Father being called a tyrant.

"Spare him," Syeron said, barely able to speak.

The older man who had fought Syeron rushed over and kicked Syeron in the mouth, knocking him down.

"Hold your tongue, filth!" he yelled, spitting next to Syeron's face in the dirt.

"Enough, Havroy," the Halvodi on the Balakar said. He got off his mount and walked toward Corrin, drawing a large, poorly made sword from his side. He stabbed it into the ground and knelt in front of Corrin, examining him.

"Your friend says I should spare you. Why? When your Father didn't show the same sentiment to our children! Our women! Our men! "

Corrin had no idea what he was talking about but answered anyway.

"My Father would never harm a woman or child, let alone without cause!"

The Halvodi let out a little laugh.

"You know nothing but lies fed to you." Havroy said, shaking his head.

"Horvric, stop toying with this fraudulent child and kill him. His presence here puts us all in danger. Kill them both!"

Syeron lifted himself back to his knees, looking as if he was going to wobble over at any moment.

"Kill me only. I was here on that day. Kill me. Don't make the boy pay for the sins of his Father."

A Halvodi woman on a Balakar next to Horvric's spoke. Her hair was long and gray. Her caramel skin glowed under the moons of Halvodon.

"The Fargulkian is right, Horvric."

She got off her mount and walked over to Syeron, drawing her sword. She put the sword on Syeron's shoulder.

"You would die for a child that is not your own?" she asked.

Syeron, using the last of his energy, turned his head to Corrin and uttered his last word. "Yes."

Corrin's eyes filled with tears. Horvric looked at Havroy, who nodded his head in an annoyed agreement. Horvric stood back up and holstered his sword. The woman raised her sword.

"I, Havrene of Halvodon, sentence you to death for the brutal crimes against our world."

Corrin let out a gut-wrenching scream as Havrene swung her sword and decapitated Syeron. Blood splattered on Corrin as Syeron's head rolled to Havroy's feet. Syeron's headless body slumped into the dirt.

Corrin's scream turned to a soundless expression. Havrene wiped off Syeron's blood on her cloak, looking at Corrin with a satisfied, but sorrowful look in her eyes. She walked back to her Balakar with Horvric.

"*Murderers. Savages. You lawless beasts!*" Corrin cried out, rivers of tears falling down his face.

He tried to stand, but the Halvodis next to him shoved him back down to his knees.

"Take the head of the Fargulkian and this boy back to Hokdro so Hirvrin can speak to him and officially decide what to do," Horvric proclaimed, settling back into the saddle of his Balakar.

A young Halvodi got off his Balakar and gave it to Havroy. He got on and rode off in formation with Horvric and Havrene. The rest began to follow. Corrin continued to yell as the Halvodis dispersed. His tears and shock made his voice crack.

"*I'll kill you. I swear, I'll kill yo—*" he yelled before getting hit in the back of the head and blacking out.

Nighttime had completely consumed Halvodon by the time Corrin woke up. The moons illuminated the land outside, as his head was killing him with pain. As he tried gathering his senses, he noticed he was inside a room.

A small fire made the area he was in warm and cozy. A table of food was set and empty. The room was filled with relics and artifacts that looked old and worn-out but that told a tale of Halvodon's past.

Corrin stood up immediately, realizing he wasn't chained or bound. He must have been out cold for what felt like hours. He was completely alone in the room and began to admire the craftsmanship of everything in there. The paintings, the table, the walls, the relics—all were different from the Halvodi savages that had captured him and killed Syeron.

"Syeron," he said quietly, placing his hands on his head while his eyes filled with tears.

As he remembered what happened to Syeron, he heard voices approaching. He darted behind the table and grabbed a knife from one of the plates as the voices entered the room. Horvric, Havroy, Havrene, and another older man walked in. Havroy drew his blade at the sight of Corrin holding the knife. The older man who Corrin hadn't seen before put his hand on Havroy's, lowering his blade.

"Havroy, please," he insisted.

"There's no need for any more blood to be spilled," he added, making his way to the table and sitting down.

Corrin watched him, still gripping his knife, as the older man began to break bread and eat.

"By all means, have a seat and join me. You must be hungry," he said, putting food in his mouth and dipping his bread into broth.

Corrin was so confused. He looked at Horvric, Havroy, and Havrene who were all not fazed by what this old man was doing.

"You may leave us. We'll be fine. We're going to have a nice chat and delicious food, aren't we?" the older man said, opening his hands over the table, signaling Corrin to sit down.

Horvric and Havrene exited the room, leaving Havroy there, glaring at Corrin, before he too exited, closing the door behind him.

"So much tension, right?," the older man joked, stuffing his face with more food.

Corrin looked back down at him, trying to figure out what this man's deal was and if he was insane or being manipulative.

"Have a seat, have a seat. It's rude to let someone eat alone."

Corrin stood for a few more seconds, deciding what to do. His stomach was growling. He hadn't eaten in hours. He finally sat down, hesitatingly at first. He slowly put the knife back down on the table.

The older man grabbed a plate and filled it with bread, broth, meat, and greens. It smelled outstanding, making Corrin's stomach rumble. The older man passed Corrin the plate.

Corrin was still nervous but felt like he could trust this man. He dug into the plate, eating all the food as if he hadn't eaten in days. The older man watched in peace as Corrin ate and enjoyed the food.

"I'm Hirvrin," he said.

Corrin continued eating rapidly, almost ignoring what Hirvrin said.

"And you are Corrin, son of Helena, son of The All Father, Heir to the Universe."

Corrin looked up slowly from his almost emptied plate. His eyes deepened with fear of the thought of what might happen next. He gulped his food and straightened out his back, trying to speak with the prestige and authority his Father raised him with.

"I am!" he said, moving his hand slowly back toward the knife.

Hirvrin saw Corrin's hand moving toward the knife and smiled, letting out a laugh.

"You are in no danger here, my boy."

Corrin took offense to that statement, remembering the events of the past few hours.

"No danger? Your people attacked us. Killed—" Corrin's voice broke as he fought back tears. "Killed my companion. My friend." Tears began to run down Corrin's face.

Hirvrin sighed, his eyes were deepened with a long history of Halvodi suffering. The sides of his head were shaved. The only hair he had was a gray mohawk tied back into a ponytail. Corrin noticed a scar on his left eye going from his forehead to his cheek. He could tell Hirvrin just had a fresh shave as well, the shadow of a thick beard still had a presence on his wrinkled face.

"I'm sorry you had to witness death in such a hard way. At such a young age. That was a taste of what happened to us. By the thousands," Hirvrin said. "By the millions."

His voice trailed off, as his eyes were lost in a state of memory. Corrin still had his eyes set on him, his tears slowly stopping. His mind raced on what exactly happened to Halvodon and its people.

Hirvrin stood up and walked to the door.

"Come with me," he said, extending a welcoming hand out to Corrin.

Corrin thought for a second, wondering if he should take the knife with him, before leaving it, walking to the door, and exiting the room with Hirvrin.

Corrin looked around as the door led them outside to a valley circled by mountains. He looked back at the door to the room and saw that it was a part of what looked to once have been a large structure.

Hirvrin saw Corrin looking at it.

"This used to be our main hall," Hirvrin uttered, joining in on examining what remained of the structure with Corrin.

"Leaders of all of Halvodon would convene here every solstice to speak on distribution of resources amongst our people. My father, his father, and his father's father before him roamed these halls."

Corrin looked at Hirvrin with sadness, feeling the pain in his voice. Hirvrin continued looking at the destroyed hall. The winds of Halvodon brushed his mohawk ponytail in the night.

"My son would have walked these halls as well. So would have my daughters, and their children after them."

Corrin saw glimmering lights in the distance. Muffled voices that sounded like children traveled by air into Corrin's ears.

"This way," Hirvrin said, following Corrin's gaze.

As they walked into a clearing, a sea of miniature campfires, huts, handcrafted tents, and hundreds of Halvodis laid before Corrin. He stood in his tracks, taking in what he was seeing.

Hirvrin continued forward.

"Welcome to Hokdro—what used to be our capital and what remains of my people."

As Corrin and Hirvrin walked through the camp, families, children, women, and men were going about their night. Many of the adults had deep, healed scars and missing limbs.

Corrin could feel their eyes on him. Children stopped playing as he walked by, looking at him with curiosity and fear. Farther down the camp, Havroy stood outside of what appeared to be his home. His two sons who had helped him attack Corrin and Syeron came outside, arms crossed. As they continued walking, Corrin began asking Hirvrin questions.

"I thought the Halvodis were advanced and civilized. This, this is—"

Hirvrin cut him off.

"Tragic?" Hirvrin asked. "We were all those things once. Halvodon was rich with all life. Our lands bloomed."

They reached the center of the camp where a large fire was lit.

"You must have been just an infant when your Father destroyed us."

Corrin looked at Hirvrin, his words piercing Corrin's soul. He tried to speak, defending his Father. But no words came out.

Hirvrin continued, "The death of your friend was a small retribution to the loss we have felt. My children and wife were gone in a blink of an eye when your Father came to Halvodon."

Hirvrin's eyes gazed at the stars in the sky.

"Centuries of Halvodi civilization were taken from us in with one swing of his Spear."

Corrin dropped to his knees. The weight of this news was too much for him to bear. He didn't want to believe what he was being told, but the evidence before him was too much to not take in Hirvrin's words.

"Our way of life was never war or killing or living like lesser beings like your Father demanded. You now know the truth, Corrin."

Corrin looked up at Hirvrin.

"The sins of your Father will not define you today. What you do with your life is up to you. And how you choose to grow into a man will be what defines you."

Hirvrin left Corrin on his knees. His words stabbed Corrin in the chest, reminding him of something similar Zaman said to him.

Hirvrin walked up to the giant fire and sat down in front of it next to Horvric and Havrene. More Halvodis began circling the fire as well. Some sitting. Some standing. Havroy appeared with his sons, and took a seat next to Hirvrin.

Corrin watched as the camp gathered around the fire and each other. They shared food and drinks. The Halvodis Corrin had read about in the book he took from Zaman were in front of him, displaying the community and fellowship that depicted this once prosperous planet.

As Corrin watched in awe, silence fell upon the camp as Havroy began humming. Men all around the fire joined in. Women and children added in a soft but fierce hymn. Hirvrin began singing:

🎵 Once there were green tall trees
a young vibrant world for all to see
no tears were fallen on leaf or stone
children laughing no person alone 🎵

The humming continued as Havrene began singing:

🎵 A time of life when mountains had breath
before our kin were led to death
from the sky whence He came
reshaping Halvodon in His name 🎵

Corrin was heartbroken listening to the song. He still couldn't believe his Father was capable of causing so much pain. As Havrene ended, the humming continued and Havroy sang:

🎵 Our men fought hard under our moons
his Spear of darkness only brought doom
once stood high our ancient halls
his power almighty destroyed it all 🎵

All the Halvodis added to the hymn. Fathers caressing daughters, mothers caressing sons. Elders looking into the fire remembering life as it used to be. Horvric began to sing:

> 🎵 Children's laughter turned to screams
> our land of old now only in our dreams
> days are long, nights are cold
> these forsaken times were never foretold🎵

The song haunted Corrin. He questioned everything he was told and taught. His life was beginning to feel like a lie. As the humming continued, Hirvrin, Havrene, Havroy, Horvric, and all the Halvodis sang together:

> 🎵 But we stand strong, our faces pale
> the voices of our ancestors sing this tale
> of green tall trees for all to see
> a vibrant world aches remember thee🎵

The moons of Halvodon glistened on the ground in front of Corrin. The humming from the Halvodis began to fade out as they dispersed to their homes. The older boy who fought Corrin earlier walked up to him.

"It gets cold here," he said, handing him a blanket.

Corrin took it. He couldn't believe how they were treating him, even after everything his Father had done to them. The older boy gave Corrin a hurt smile, hurt more so for Corrin's realization rather than his own suffering.

As the older boy walked away, Corrin yelled out to him, "What's your name?"

He turned back to Corrin with eyes friendlier than before.

"Hivli, after my grandfather."

Corrin stood up, wrapped himself in the blanket, and walked up to Hivli, extending his hand.

"Thank you. And I'm sorry."

Hivli extended his hand to Corrin, locking arms and symbolizing a new future between possible friends.

As Hivli was about to say something a loud crack was heard in the sky. Something broke the atmosphere. Halvodis exited their homes and looked up into the clouds.

Children dropped their toys and ran to their parents. Corrin and Hivli stared at the clouds as a zooming light ripped through the air.

Hirvrin whispered, "No."

The light hit the ground, shaking the mountains and launching back Halvodis who were close to the impact. Havroy came running up to Corrin and Hivli.

"Take your brother back to the house *now!*"

Havroy darted off with Horvric and other Halvodi men. Hivli ran off to get his brother. As the dust settled from the impact, Corrin's eyes widened at the sight of his Father.

Woman and children began screaming. The Halvodis ran in every direction, terrified that The All Father had returned.

The All Father was wielding the Spear of Space and began evaporating any Halvodi he saw. Men came at him on their Balakars and were immediately turned to ash by the Spear.

"Where is *my son?*" The All Father yelled, flying up into the air and zooming back down, sending a blast and shock wave that blew away the homes of the Halvodis.

The blast sent Corrin back, knocking him out. He woke up a few minutes later to all the structures on fire. His vision was blurry and his hearing fuzzy. Screams of women were heard all around him. Children were crying.

He stood up, still dizzy from the blast. He saw his Father blasting Halvodis away. In the distance he saw Hivli and his little brother holding what remained of their father, Havroy, with tears and screams coming out of them.

Corrin stumbled to his Father, walking over the bodies of dead Halvodis. Children were crying over their parents' lifeless corpses. Mothers were holding their dead babies, yelling out with pain Corrin never imagined.

Horvric was on his knees holding Havrene's dying body in his arms. His screams were shattering. As Corrin got closer to his towering Father, he saw Hirvrin under his Father's foot.

Hirvrin saw Corrin staring at him. His face covered in blood, he mouthed to Corrin, "Choose your own way," before The All Father pierced him in the head with the Spear of Space.

Corrin stood in the midst of the death and destruction, numb by it all. The All Father finally noticed him and ran up to him, his thick black cloak following behind. He bolted the Spear into the ground and grabbed Corrin by the shoulders.

"My son."

He looked Corrin up and down, making sure he wasn't injured in any way. Multiple ships from The Black Palace began to emerge from the atmosphere, descending onto the land. Platoons of Black Palace soldiers exited, firing upon any Halvodi still alive.

"They all will die for what they did to you." The All Father proclaimed, while the sound of blasters and more screaming could be heard.

"Where is Syeron? Is he hurt?"

Corrin was still in shock at everything that had just happened. He looked up at his Father's deep white eyes.

"Syeron is dead, Father."

The All Father let go of Corrin. He turned away from him, out of sadness and anger.

"Everything I do, I do for you. For your future. For a kingdom that will be yours. An empire you can pass down to my kin," The All Father said. "Because of your childish games, Syeron is dead."

Corrin stood silent. Screams of the Halvodis began to wither out. All that was left were the wails of mothers and fatherless children.

Black Palace troops approached The All Father and Corrin. Their metallic black armor glimmered under the moonlight. The All Father's seal shone on their chests as energy swords glowed from their belts.

"Head home, son. We will deal with your foolishness once I return."

The Black Palace troops escorted Corrin safely to one of the ships, shooting anyone still alive. Corrin entered the ship and looked around one last time at the now completely destroyed Hokdro. The capital of Halvodon was no more.

In the distance Corrin saw Hivli and his little brother still holding Havroy's body. Hivli glared at Corrin before cutting his eyes away. Corrin's heart sank to the bottom of his stomach as the hatch door closed.

While the ship ascended into the clouds, Black Palace troops circled the remaining survivors of the Halvodi people. Through the glass of the ship Corrin could hear his Father's voice from the ground.

"My mercy will never be taken for granted again."

As the ship left the atmosphere, Corrin's last image of Halvodon was met with a large, soundless blast from the Spear of Space.

Corrin slumped down into his seat, his head aching from everything. A ward on the ship approached him.

"Would you like anything to eat?" the ward asked.

CHAPTER 3

DANGEROUS WINDS AHEAD

"Are we really going into that?" a young soldier asked nervously, sweat trickling down his neck.

He was probably about sixteen years old. A fresh recruit from Gorkon, a small mining planet close to The Black Palace. The young soldier was standing on the edge of a carrier ship with more soldiers—some new recruits and others aged in the art of warfare.

"Shut your mouth," a large man said, who appeared to be a commanding officer.

His black armor was more worn-out and used than the other soldiers. The All Father's seal, the orb of the Spear of Space, was imprinted on his chest plate.

The commanding officer was Fargulkian, as most commanding officers were. His massive size intimidated his soldiers.

"You'll do as you are told. When he steps foot on this platform, hold your tongues and keep your eyes forward."

Below them roared the strength of a thousand men, rebels on the planet Pugart. Pugart had once been a staunch ally of The Black Palace, but after years of its leaders subsidizing the planet's resources to the elite, the rest of the planet had revolted, killing the puppet leaders put in place by The All Father. The rebels had taken out numerous Black Palace strongholds in a swift campaign of reclaiming the planet for themselves.

Back on the platform, the young recruits were terrified at the sound of the men below them. Inside the carrier ship, Corrin sat. It had been ten years since the events of Halvodon. His hair was long and thick, just like his mother's. Black strands from his mane blew in his face. His eyes told a story of campaign after campaign, mission after mission. Battles sparked to squash any noise of rebellion against his Father.

The years since Halvodon had been crucial to Corrin's growth. His complete loyalty and alignment with The All Father put him at the head of the military, earning him respect and fear from friend and foe alike. His name spread across the entire universe like wildfire, due to his successes and viciousness on the battlefield.

Something in Corrin had changed after that night on Halvodon. The man he grew into was a dark version of the boy he once was. His lack of empathy, mercy, and patience in war earned him the nickname The Shepherd of Fire, a nickname that impressed The All Father. The nickname and approval from his Father spiraled him deeper into The All Father's grasp.

Corrin stood up from his seat in the carrier. The yelling from outside, below the ship, was drowned out by his thoughts. To him this was another rebellion to be put out. On the end of the carrier platform were the new recruits—he knew most weren't going to make it home.

As he stepped onto the platform, the sun of Pugart blasted him in the face, making him squint. Soldiers looked at him in awe, respect, and fear as he made his way to the edge of the platform.

The young recruit from Gorkon gulped as Corrin passed him. His metallic armor glistened in the sunlight. The crimson red trim of his armor had been through so many battles in the past ten years, but it still had a shine on it as if it was brand-new.

The wind from the ship hovering over Pugart made Corrin's long dark brown cape dance on its own, immortalizing Corrin to the soldiers behind him. He looked down at Pugart, studying the rebels.

They were disorganized. No battle formations. No structural leadership. But their rage and passion to be free of The All Father was heard in their yells. Their willingness to die for their cause stood out more than any valor or coordination ever could.

Corrin looked to the sun of Pugart, letting the sunrays hit his face. The warmth reminded him of his youth and summers with his Father. A time that would never be again.

He turned to the soldiers behind him and spoke, "Some of you will die today. Some of you will make it home to your mothers and fathers. The blood you shed today will rain down forever in history as courageous men who fought for The Black Palace. Fight and die. Or fight and live."

Corrin finished his speech by jumping off the platform, leaving the new recruits, especially the young soldier from Gorkon, in shock.

"Did he just…?" the young soldier muttered.

The commanding officer put on his helmet and whipped out his energy sword.

"Follow the Shepherd," he yelled.

The soldiers put down the face masks on their helmets and readied themselves to jump as the carrier ship rapidly descended toward the battlefield.

As Corrin flew to the ground of Pugart, the rebels began to shoot at him. Some of them had blasters, others arrows. The Pugarts were known to lace their arrows with poison that instantly paralyzed and killed an enemy once it touched flesh.

As the blasters and arrows zoomed past Corrin, he pulled out his sword and landed the blade on the head of a rebel, splitting him in two. In the sky, the carrier ship unloaded the soldiers. They jumped down, hitting the ground and quickly thrusting themselves into battle.

Some were killed before exiting the platform, their bodies falling off and smashing into the dirt as the carrier ship ascended back into the clouds.

Corrin raced through the rebels, taking on dozens of them at once. His sword ripped through their bones easily. Their low-tier armor was no match for his strength and blade.

Around him, Black Palace soldiers and rebels fought hard, the shuffling of feet and war made the battlefield a sea of yellow, as the dirt below them rose in the air. Blood splattered in every direction. Corrin continued ripping through the rebels, trying to find who was leading the battle on their side.

The Pugarts' rebellion was so completely unstructured that intelligence from Black Palace sources on the ground beforehand had a tough time figuring out who was in charge. From the distance, and over the screams and grunts, Corrin heard a raspy voice yell, *"Focus on the son. Take him out!"*

Corrin saw the man amongst the battle, killing Black Palace soldiers. He was young and taller than Corrin. He had tattoos all over his body. His bald head was covered in sweat and blood. His beard was dripping with sweat. Corrin knew he must be the one leading the rebels.

As the rebel leader yelled, dozens upon dozens of rebels charged Corrin. He launched them back, splitting them open with his sword, but there were too many of them. As they piled on him, trying to blast and stab him, Corrin knelt down and shot himself into the air.

Some of the rebels were still holding on to him as he flew up into the clouds and back down to the ground. The shock wave launched the rebels away in all directions, killing them instantly.

Energy began forming around Corrin's sword and open hand. The young soldier from Gorkon watched in awe as Corrin, The Shepherd of Fire, spun and blasted rebels away. His sword turned rebels into charred bodies on contact.

After Halvodon, The All Father was furious with Corrin's childish curiosity. He was angry that Corrin's interest in Halvodon had led to Syeron being killed, but what really made The All Father rage was that Corrin wasn't able to defend himself or kill the Halvodis on his own. So, he sent Corrin back out to continue his studies and made sure he was turned into a formidable warrior.

His studies abroad shifted from cultural understanding to military and tactical knowledge. His itinerary of planets to visit were changed to the most brutal worlds that taught Corrin how to be an instinctive killer.

One planet, Ovaseryn, introduced Corrin to the cosmic arts and taught him how to channel the energy that was naturally inside him due to the spears.

The Ovaseryns, and many planets alike, learned how to channel energy inside them through the stars and other ways. Life-forms who mastered the cosmic arts were more powerful than most beings but still no match for Corrin or The All Father.

Black Palace soldiers protected the wounded while Corrin made his way to the leader of the rebels. Most of the rebels began running from the sight of Corrin heading their way. His power and intensity crushed their spirits after witnessing in person the stories they'd heard of his ferocity.

As Corrin approached the rebel leader, the tall, bald, bearded Pugart sprinted at him. The surrounding rebels and Black Palace soldiers stopped fighting to watch.

The rebel leader swung his blade at Corrin, missing as Corrin effortlessly evaded him. Worn-out from swinging and missing, the rebel leader hunched over, catching his breath.

Corrin looked around and took in the calmness of the battle. Rebels and Black Palace soldiers alike were looking at him, anticipating his next move. He noticed that most of the rebels were very young. Others were old. Fathers, sons, workers, civilians of Pugart fighting for their homes and lives. The faces of these rebels shook Corrin.

He thought, *These aren't rebels or soldiers, they're people…* His moment of forgetting he was in the middle of a battle was cut short as the rebel leader came at him again.

Corrin was caught by surprise and reacted, dodging the blow to his face and striking the leader in the stomach. His sword ripped through the rebel leader's flesh, exiting through his back.

The rebel leader's eyes widened. He gasped for air as Corrin slowly pulled out his sword. As the rebel leader collapsed to the ground, Corrin looked into his eyes. He could see the life slipping away from the leader, death taking him to meet all the others slain by Corrin's blade.

Corrin looked around again. All eyes were on him, making him feel uneasy for the first time in a while. The other rebels began dropping their weapons and surrendering. Ten years of being molded by death and war turned him into a stone-cold killer, but today he felt his skin crawl. It was the same feeling he felt back on Halvodon as a boy.

"What should we do with the rest of the rebels?" asked the Fargulkian commanding officer.

Corrin was still inside his head, his thoughts racing.

"Sir?" the commanding officer asked.

Corrin snapped out of the trance he was in and replied, "The battle is won, Dyerian."

Corrin then floated into the air and addressed the rebels.

"Return to your homes. This battle is over!"

As he descended to the ground, he began walking away.

Dyerian rushed over to him, saying, "Corrin, our orders were to wipe out the rebels completely. The All Father—"

Corrin cut him off. "The All Father is not here, Dyerian, I am. These people will return to their homes. Enough blood has been shed today."

Dyerian glared at him with his dark Fargulkian eyes, unamused at the compassion Corrin was showing. He had witnessed Corrin commit atrocities in the name of The All Father and was unsure why this battle was any different.

For years Dyerian had stood in Corrin's shadow, rising through the ranks of The Black Palace military, only to be sidelined every time just because he wasn't the son of the creator. After Halvodon, Corrin was thrown into the midst of harsher training, with Dyerian right by his side. Together they grew and became formidable warriors, with Corrin always a step ahead.

Corrin made his way across the battlefield. Pugart rebels were scavenging through the dead, looking for survivors. Black Palace soldiers were carrying their wounded back to the carrier ships as medics checked to see if the wounds were fatal or not. Across the field, the young recruit from Gorkon laid lifeless on the ground with rebel arrows sticking out from all sides of him.

Back in The Black Palace, wards awaited Corrin's return from Pugart. A feast was prepared for the victory. Emissaries and diplomats from the planetary kingdom were arriving to join Corrin and The All Father.

After every victory, The All Father threw a massive ball to magnify the glory of his son's successes on the battlefield. Most guests came for the sheer points and bragging rights of being in The All Father's presence, while others came out of fear of not wanting The All Father to turn on them.

As Corrin entered the atmosphere of The Black Palace, his ship docked in its usual spot. An assembly of troops and generals were outside already, waiting to give him praise. He was met with applause and grand gestures of gratitude by wards, guards, and Black Palace women.

When Corrin was young, The All Father took the most beautiful women of every planet in his empire and brought them to The Black Palace to live. They were meant to bring pleasure and peace to the realm of The All Father, but some say they were there to fill The All Father's void of losing Helena.

Entering the massive halls, Corrin felt all eyes on him again. Blood, dirt, and sweat painted his armor and face. Women from different worlds were laying all around the Palace, eating and drinking, admiring him as he went to his room.

His room was on the upper level of The Black Palace. Its windows gave Corrin a clear view of space. His balcony allowed him to step outside into the sea of stars and peer into the far reaches of the universe.

As Corrin removed his armor and undressed, he caught a glimpse of himself in a mirror. His dirt-covered face showed a young man lost in his Father's shadow. A scar from a previous battle stretched from his forehead down through his white eye to his cheek. He continued to look at himself, trying to find any sign of the boy he used to be as a ward came in.

"Sorry to bother you, Corrin, but your Father requests an audience with you immediately."

Corrin sighed. "I'll be right there."

He washed himself off briefly and put on a long robe, letting his bare chest out. Minor battle scars were littered across his body, showcasing the years of training and battles his Father had put him through. The robe dragged across The Black Palace floors as Corrin made his way to The All Father's chambers.

A grand spiral staircase led to The All Father's room at the tip of The Black Palace. Voices inside could be heard as Corrin approached.

"Corrin? Is that you?" The All Father's voice boomed behind the closed doors.

Wards inside the chamber opened the gigantic doors for Corrin as he walked in. The All Father's chamber was a massive circular dome with tall intimidating statues of himself. Wards, advisors, and diplomats from other worlds filled the area. They watched in awe as the son of the creator entered.

Across the room, The All Father walked toward Corrin. He pushed through the guests, grabbing Corrin's face abruptly. He turned Corrin's head left to right.

"Good, no wounds," The All Father said, walking to a massive chair in the room.

Corrin rubbed his face, annoyed that every time he came back from battle his Father checked to see if he was wounded or not.

As The All Father sat in his chair, a ward brought him a goblet. Its size was suited for the creator of all.

"Father, what is it you summoned me for?" Corrin asked, gesturing *no thank you* to a ward that was bringing him something to drink.

The All Father scoffed before taking a sip of his drink, then answered. "I have to have a reason to see my own son? Why do you always think I have an agenda, Corrin?"

Corrin rolled his eyes and tried not to laugh. He knew his Father only summoned him for something important like a mission or new battle plans. The All Father finished his drink, set the glass down, stood up, and ordered everyone in the room to leave.

"Leave us. I must speak to my son alone."

As everyone exited, The All Father made his way toward another staircase.

"Come," The All Father demanded, his tone sterner now.

Corrin was confused. The staircase led to the roof of The Black Palace, the highest point where The All Father's throne and the Spear of Space rested. The roof was in open space, giving a clear view of the vastness of the entire universe. Corrin followed his Father up the staircase, wondering why they were going up there.

The All Father had his arms behind his back. His dark blue skin glistened in the darkness of space as trillions of stars shone down upon him. With his back still to Corrin, he spoke, "Do I neglect you, son?"

Corrin was taken aback by the question.

"What? No, Father, of course not," he answered, stumbling over his words.

"Have I not given you everything, my son?" The All Father asked, turning now to face Corrin, his hands still behind his back, his body towering over him.

Corrin was nervous. "Yes, Father, you have. What is this about?" Corrin asked, concerned with what The All Father was going to do.

The All Father glared at Corrin with his piercing white eyes. Corrin stared back with his green-and-white eyes. The All Father then circled Corrin, sizing him up, before walking to the throne. As he reached the throne, he put his hand on the Spear. Corrin's eyes widened. Then The All Father removed his hand from the Spear and sat down.

He sighed. "My son, when I ask you to do something, do it. The rebels on Pugart were to be wiped out completely. Not left alive."

Corrin's body relaxed, the tension from a few seconds earlier was relieved by his Father's tone.

"I understand you have compassion for these mortals, but these rebels now think they can do whatever they want without facing dire consequences," The All Father said, putting his hand on his head.

Corrin stepped forward. "Father, the rebel leader was defeated, their morale was—"

The All Father cut him off with a scoff. He stabbed Corrin with a fierce glare. "Enough, enough, enough, You're the Shepherd of Fire, not the Shepherd of Mercy. When I send you in my name to reclaim what is mine, and yours by birthright, I expect you to execute my orders directly, as is, without question. When you sit on this throne, then you can make your own decisions on the battlefield. Until then, it is I who sits on this throne. It is I who yields the Spear of Space, and it is my word that will be followed, undoubtedly!"

Corrin tried to speak, but The All Father raised his hand.

"Do not speak. Listen. Your tongue has already caused enough damage today."

Corrin clenched his jaw. He was mad because he knew Dyerian must have complained to The All Father.

"I've already sent Dyerian back with a small team to eradicate the rebels. *All* of them. No Pugart who fought against my kingdom will live to see their sun rise in the morning," The All Father said, glaring out into the far reaches of space.

Corrin was struck with grief. All he could remember was the faces of the young rebels.

"Why wasn't I informed? I lead your armies, don't I? I had the right to be made aware!" Corrin claimed, his voice raised.

The All Father stood, yelling, "You have a right because I say you do. Any right you have, any right my creations have, is because of my *willingness to allow it*!"

His voice boomed into the universe.

Below in The Black Palace, the women and wards shook in fear. The All Father walked toward Corrin, then walked back to his throne, aggressively sitting down.

He spoke to Corrin, his voice more relaxed now.

"Ready your ship. You are to head to Rashalon tonight."

Corrin was still in shock at his Father's powerful voice yelling at him, but answered him. "Rashalon?

What for? They aren't at war with us," Corrin said, completely confused as to why he was being sent there.

"You want to use your tongue to end battles? You think you're a diplomat? Here's your chance to prove it. Rashalon, as you know, is one of our strongest loyalists. Due to their loyalty, I allow them to appoint a new viceroy every five years. They appointed a new one yesterday, Viceroy Tirus. Rumors say he's an idealist. Apparently, he's been known to have 'anti-Father' sentiments."

Corrin was unimpressed. His missions were on the battlefield.

"OK, and what do you want me to do?" Corrin asked, trying to figure out his Father's plan.

"You will go in my place to the Viceroy Gala. Get a feel for this man. Report back to me. I need to know if he will be a threat to my rule in Rashalon."

The All Father stood and walked toward Corrin, placing his hands on his shoulders.

"Corrin, we are entering into a time of peace. The rebels on Pugart will be extinguished by morning. My worlds will finally be under my generous rule, together as one planetary kingdom. I need to make sure this new viceroy does not have any plans to ruin what I—what we—have built."

Corrin was looking at the throne, then he looked at his Father, whose white eyes convinced him to go ahead and go.

"I am your son, Father, and what you command, I shall do," Corrin recited, letting out a smile.

The All Father held Corrin a little longer, giving Corrin the hope that his Father was going to embrace him, something he can barely remember his Father ever doing. The All Father removed his hands and walked back to the throne.

"Leave at once to Rashalon. The gala is tomorrow night, but the viceroy is expecting an audience with me, well you, tonight."

Corrin bowed his head and headed back to the stairs to leave.

"And, Corrin, do not forget, all of this will one day be yours."

Corrin gave his Father a weak smile. He hurried down the stairs and made his way to his chambers to get ready to travel to Rashalon.

Across the stars, past the deepest reaches of The All Father's mapped-out rule, Zaman sat in his Sanctuary of Time, organizing all the millions of events he had recorded throughout his existence. His massive sanctuary was grand and vast, sitting alone in the sea of space. The lone structure was made out of metal and stone, littered with energy from the Spears. It resembled that of a watchtower, suitable for the Time Keeper.

As Zaman shuffled through towers of records, a gust of wind fluttered his long cloak. When he turned to see where the wind came from, he heard a low whisper ring out his name.

"Zaman," echoed throughout the sanctuary, bouncing off the books and walls.

He stood up and searched the sanctuary, confused as to where the voice was coming from. When he entered his private chambers, an eerie aura, or essence, consumed him. He was immediately drawn to the Spear of Time, which rested in a gigantic glass case in the middle of the room.

The Spear of Time radiated a bright light Zaman had never seen before. The radiating glow captivated him, drawing Zaman closer to the Spear in a state of trance and concern. As he reached the glass case, he opened it and pulled the Spear out. Holding the Spear with both hands, Zaman spoke into it.

"Nox?"

Back in The Black Palace, The All Father was still sitting on his throne, thinking about his conversation with Corrin and the future of the universe. As he sat, he heard Zaman's voice.

The All Father's eyes widened. He looked around, searching for the Time Keeper.

Searching for the origin of the voice, he turned his head slowly to the Spear of Space that was radiating an aura The All Father had never seen before. As he moved closer to the Spear, he heard his real name again.

"Nox. Are you there?"

The All Father was dumbfounded by what was happening. He grabbed the Spear and held it for a second before drawing it close to his face and whispering back, "Zaman?"

Zaman was shocked to hear The All Father speak to him through the Spear. He answered him back, "Nox, we've never been able to do this."

The All Father stood in the vastness of space, intrigued and confused as to how he and Zaman were able to communicate through the Spears like this.

Back in the Sanctuary of Time, Zaman continued, "Cycles of being heralds for the Spears, and we are now being shown that there's more to them—us—than we imagined. This is outstanding."

The All Father listened to Zaman, considering this achievement a step forward in his personal goals and possibly a new way to gather the entire universe under his control.

"How is this possible, Zaman?" The All Father asked, wanting to know more.

"I don't know, Nox, the Spear called out to me, as if it were you."

Zaman began to think, trying to piece this all together. The All Father continued to let his mind race, romanticizing what this could mean for his empire.

"I'm going to study this, Nox. The potential to learn more about why we were created, why the Spears chose us, seems closer than ever now."

The All Father's eyes glistened with power.

"Let me know what you find, brother," The All Father said, his tone chilling to Zaman's ears.

Zaman immediately dived into his studies, searching for anything the Spear had revealed to him throughout his existence as the Time Keeper.

In The Black Palace, The All Father stared deeply into the Spear of Space, yearning for more answers and power.

"Show me our destiny," The All Father whispered.

CHAPTER 4

THE RIDER OF RASHALON

Corrin entered his ship's common room, tired from the battle on Pugart and weary of his long trip to Rashalon in place of his Father.

"So, the Father has you doing diplomatic work now, huh, Corrin?" joked a man sitting down.

Corrin dropped onto a seat in the common room and laid on his back, covering his eyes with his arms. He peeked out and replied, "Doesn't seem like much diplomacy if you're here."

The rest of the crew laughed. The man playfully threw a piece of bread at Corrin, hitting him in the chest.

"Thanks," Corrin responded, grabbing the bread and taking a bite out of it.

The man was named Grater and has been one of Corrin's best friends since childhood. He came to The Black Palace with his mother and father, who left their home on the asteroid colonies of Braroclyn. His parents had sought work as wards for The All Father and have been in The Black Palace ever since.

Grater's black skin shone under the ship's interior lights. His dreads slightly covered his yellow eyes. He was a little shorter than Corrin but was one of the toughest people Corrin had ever met. He and Corrin had traveled all over the universe together on missions, adventures, and, of course, leisure.

"Grater, you being on this highly important mission of peace is a sham. The second you open your mouth, we're all dead," joked a woman as she entered the common room.

Corrin stood, laughing at the woman's joke. She smiled at Corrin. A shy smile of hidden flirtation and possibly love. Her slender build was armored with a black chest plate and black arm guards. Her long legs were smooth and strong. She looked at Corrin with her piercing blue eyes that were exposed by her tied-back blonde hair.

Corrin nervously tried not to make eye contact with her. Their history of growing up together and having a brief relationship was still on his mind. Her name was Moira and she had been born in The Black Palace to a military family highly respected by The All Father. Their relationship seemed like a perfect match to anyone on the outside but not to Corrin.

"We will be arriving shortly to Rashalon, sir," yelled one of the pilots from the cockpit.

Corrin gave Moira a half smile and walked off to his personal quarters to prepare. Grater looked at Moira, who was left in the dust of Corrin quickly leaving to avoid her, and giggled.

Corrin sat in his quarters dressed in Black Palace garments. His armor rested on the floor beside his bed. He sat in silence, thinking of the faces of the rebels on Pugart. His memory of being on Halvodon and seeing what his Father had done to the Halvodis haunted him. He could still see Hivli's face. As Corrin continued peering into his mind, there was a knock at his door. Grater walked in.

"We're entering Rashalon's atmosphere. Are you ready?"

Corrin rubbed his eyes and stood up.

As he walked to the door, Grater stopped him. Grater looked intensely into Corrin's eyes.

"You good, man? You've been acting strange. What happened on Pugart?!"

Corrin hesitated for a second, remembering the faces of the Halvodis again, and the faces of the young rebels on Pugart.

"Corrin? Are you okay?"

Grater tried to put his hand on Corrin's shoulders, but Corrin pushed it away.

"I'm fine. Just tired. Let's get this over with."

Corrin stormed off, leaving Grater confused.

As Corrin and Grater entered the common room of the ship, Moira was there ready with the rest of the crew and Corrin's detail team.

"The Rashos have been a true ally of The Black Palace for years now. This is only a diplomatic mission to ensure their new viceroy continues a strong allegiance with The All Father. Myself, Grater, Moira, and my guards will heed the new viceroy's invitation for a private audience tonight, and the morning after the Gala, we will make way back to The Black Palace."

As Corrin exited the ship, the green landscape of Rashalon fascinated him. In the distance, giant waterfalls rushed to the ground.

"Beautiful, isn't it?" Moira said to Corrin, smiling.

Corrin kept admiring the planet in awe.

"Yes, it is," he replied, ignoring once again Moira's flirtatious advances.

"So, this is the Shepherd of Fire we've all heard so much about?" said a voice.

Corrin and his team all turned their heads. In front of them was an escort team of about twenty men. They were in dark green armor with tan cloaks flowing in the wind. All of them were mounted on sleek, four-legged riding creatures called Vasari. The escort teams heads were protected by helmets the same color of their armor and their eyes were shaded away from the rim.

Two of the riders were holding flags with The All Father's insignia and the seal of Rashalon's native culture. Corrin stepped forward, his cloak dragging in the dirt.

"I am Corrin of The Black Palace. Son of Helena. Son of The All Father."

There was a twinge of hostility in the air. Silence took hold. Moira gripped her sword and shield, as Grater placed his hands on the blasters strapped to his side. The tension was broken as one of the riders, who sounded like a female, spoke.

"Welcome to Rashalon, Corrin."

The rider speaking lifted their hand and, from the back of the escort team, armored individuals brought forward Vasaris.

"The viceroy is waiting for you," the rider said.

Corrin, Grater, and Moira mounted their Vasaris and followed the escort team.

The capital of Rashalon was filled with street vendors, merchants yelling, kids running around, and All Father posters exemplifying his reign and all the good he does for the universe. Some were ripped and vandalized.

People of Rashalon had never seen Corrin, but they sensed he was of importance. They stared at him. Some threw flowers and waved while others glared and walked away in disgust.

"Sentiments seem particularly at odds, eh?" Grater noted to Corrin.

The guards walking behind them were armed and ready to attack if things got out of hand. As Moira passed a little shop, a young Rasho girl ran up to her Vasari and handed her a necklace. Corrin smirked at Moira who was shocked.

As they approached a grand building with massive stone pillars and large stairs, the escort team got off their Vasaris. Corrin and his friends did the same. The rider who spoke earlier came up to Corrin, their helmet level with his chin.

"This way," they said.

The moon of Rashalon began to rise behind the building as night settled over the planet.

Inside the building, the escort team dispersed. The building was beautiful inside. Paintings on the ceiling depicted Rashalon's history. Statues of men and women immortalized leaders of the past. Corrin took it all in, remembering as a boy he loved learning about the cultures and histories of other worlds. His moment of remembrance was broken by the rider.

"The viceroy will see you now, Shepherd of Fire."

The guards waited as Corrin, Moira, and Grater followed the rider into a large room. The room was loaded with books, maps, and art. A table was littered with what looked like letters and invoices. The room was cluttered and did not look like a room appropriate enough for the arrival of The All Father or his son.

As Corrin and his friends waited, a man came stumbling out from behind a bookcase. His hair was ruffled. He carried dozens of books stacked together. He was scrawny and had a frail physique.

As he kicked shut the bookcase, the books he was carrying began to fall. Corrin rushed over. The rider stepped forward but stopped as they saw Corrin helping the man.

"Beasts of old, clumsy me," the man joked.

As Corrin picked up one of the books, he smiled.

"*The Codex of Grand Master Kilios of Noplia*. Fantastic book," Corrin said, walking the man and his books to the cluttered table. The man set the books down.

"You've read it?" the man asked, his eyes lighting up.

"Read it? I adored that book growing up. Kilios was a fantastic orator and philosopher. I wish I could have met him," Corrin said.

The man laughed, his older age becoming more noticeable to Corrin.

"Yes, yes. A formidable man he was. The Itarians had brilliant minds. Corrupted ones as well. But Kilios, oh he was brilliant. Died long before you were born, my child."

The man walked around the table and sat down. The rider was standing with their hands behind their back. The man gestured for Corrin, Moira, and Grater to sit with him.

"Sit please."

As they sat, Moira looked over to the rider who was just standing there.

"Welcome to Rashalon. I am Viceroy Tirus", the man said, smiling.

"You're the viceroy?!" Grater blurted out.

Corrin glared at him.

Grater mouthed "sorry" and sank into his seat.

Tirus laughed. "Yes. I do not seem like your ordinary leader, but Rashalon was in need of someone whose vision for a better world comes not from their appearance of being strong and full of might but from their mind and soul."

These words struck Corrin, penetrating his subconscious.

"Excuse my companion, Viceroy. He's uneducated in formal settings such as this," Corrin said, giving Grater the side-eye.

"It is OK, Corrin. I too was once young and curious. Coming from the hard streets of Rashalon made me realize that the most unrefined versions of us are the purest form of who we are. So, nice to meet you as well…" the viceroy said, looking at Grater.

"Oh, Grater, sir. The name is Grater," he responded, straightening out his sitting posture.

"Ah, Grater. Powerful name. Named after the crater made from the moon that devastated Jargun-Ba."

"Yes," Grater said enthusiastically and surprised that Tirus knew that.

"And who is this lovely lady in our presence?" Tirus asked.

"Moira of The Black Palace, Viceroy," Moira responded.

"Moira. A beautiful name for a beautiful woman," Tirus said.

Moira blushed.

"I see you've met Commander Evrii, leader of Rashalon's security forces," Tirus stated, pointing at the rider who brought Corrin and his friends inside.

The rider walked over, taking off their helmet and revealing a woman. Corrin was struck by her immense beauty.

Her long black hair swayed down over the shoulders of her armor. Her fair skin glowed under the illuminating moonlight shimmering through the viceroy's office window. She had light purple eyes that sang to Corrin.

He had never seen someone as gorgeous or lovely, yet as fierce, as her. He stood immediately. Moira, Grater, and Tirus looked at him as he introduced himself.

"Commander, pleasure to meet you. I am Corrin of The—"

She cut him off, "Black Palace. Yes, Shepherd of Fire, we all know who you are!" she said sternly.

Corrin was shocked to see how quickly she shut him down but also extremely captivated and interested.

Evrii turned to Viceroy Tirus.

"If I am no longer needed here, sir, I will retire to my chambers," she said, her voice soft and strong, lingering in Corrin's ear, making him want more.

"Of course, Commander, thank you," Tirus said.

As she left, Corrin stared at her walking away. She closed the door, and they locked eyes for a second before she was gone. Moira glared enviously at Corrin as he turned back to face the viceroy.

"A strong, loyal, and captivating woman she is," Tirus said, picking up on Corrin's admiration for Evrii.

"Yes, she is," Corrin whispered.

"Now, the reason for this meeting," the viceroy exerted, standing up and walking to the door. Opening it, he continued, "If your companions would be so happy as to head to their guest chambers, that would be appreciated greatly."

A few wards walked in.

Grater and Moira looked at Corrin, who gestured them to go.

"Great," Tirus said. "Take Corrin's companions to their chambers and show them the hospitality we Rashos have to offer."

As the door closed, Tirus walked back to his seat and sat down. Corrin was still mesmerized by Commander Evrii but focused on what the meeting between him and Viceroy Tirus was about.

"Corrin," the viceroy said, speaking first. "Were you sent here in place of The All Father, or did you decide to come on your own accord?"

Corrin was taken aback by this question, and chose his words wisely.

He cleared his throat. "I believe it's my duty to understand the importance of diplomacy and who all live in the empire," Corrin said.

"Serve," Tirus said.

"Excuse me?" Corrin asked, confused.

"Serve. Who all *serve* in the empire."

Corrin didn't know how to answer. He felt a nervous sweat trickling down his ear.

"We, the people of Rashalon, and the other worlds, serve the empire. Calling it *living* is a fancy word," Tirus said, sitting back in his seat and crossing his legs.

Corrin couldn't tell what Tirus was up to, but he remembered his Father telling him about certain sentiments Tirus had. Corrin finally gathered his thoughts and responded back to Tirus.

"The empire offers a chance for a unified kingdom that cuts the cost of trade, allowing medicine, food, supplies, and resources to travel between worlds with the guarantee of arrival. My Fa—, The All Father, protects his creations and only asks for loyalty in return!" Corrin exclaimed.

"Yes, you're right, Corrin. The empire ensures the survival of materialistic items from point A to point B. Items that do help obedient bodies of the empire. Just like the Itarian empire before. But what about those who don't obey? Those who don't want to serve The All Father's empire?" Tirus said, leaning in.

As Corrin sat in his chair, he could feel anger rushing up from his feet to his stomach to his head.

"What about them?!" Corrin exclaimed.

He began to remember the faces of the Halvodis, of the Pugarts, and all the others who were slaughtered for not obeying The All Father's desire to form a planetary kingdom.

Tirus could see Corrin was getting uncomfortable and sat back in his seat.

"Rashalon wants to enter into a new phase of peace, with The All Father, in accordance with The Black Palace," Tirus said.

Corrin felt a sigh of relief.

"But we ask only one thing," Tirus said.

Corrin straightened himself out. "And that is?" he asked.

"The complete eradication of Rasho boys being conscripted into The All Father's army." Tirus stared at Corrin, waiting for his reaction and answer.

Corrin pondered the thought. He knew that most conscripts were young and never made it home after their first campaign. He looked outside the window of Tirus's office, wondering if true peace would ever fall upon the universe.

He looked back at Tirus, whose eyes told a tale of wanting freedom and safety for all his people.

"I will bring these matters up to The All Father once I return back to The Black Palace," Corrin said.

Tirus smiled.

"That's all we want. An open dialogue to ensure the continued peace between our planets and people," Tirus said, standing.

Corrin stood also, trying to brush off the feeling of shame he felt from representing years of bloodshed.

Tirus extended his hand. "Go rest now, Corrin. We'll see each other again tomorrow night at the Gala."

Corrin shook his hand and left the room. Wards guided him to his guest chambers where he fell into a deep sleep.

Nightmares plagued Corrin's dreams that night. Faces of those he murdered in the name of The All Father glared at him. Fear crept into his body. He had no idea what was going on with him and why he was being plagued with seeing these ghosts. Sun from outside his room danced behind the shades.

I must have overslept, he thought.

Traditional Rasho garments rested on a pedestal near the door. He rose from his bed, stretched his body, and opened the blinds. The sun of Rashalon hit his skin, giving Corrin a sense of hope for the future, squashing the fears of his visions for only a moment.

As he left his guest chambers, Grater and Moira were already waiting for him outside.

"Late night?" Grater teasingly asked Corrin as he approached.

"Needed some rest," Corrin responded.

"Moira," Corrin said, greeting her.

Moira was dressed in a traditional Rasho two-piece. The garments shaped her body magnificently, making Corrin almost miss the intimate nights they used to spend together. She smiled and blushed at him staring at her.

"These pieces of cloth do itch and air out places I'd rather not say," Grater mumbled, tugging and scratching at the Rasho garments he was wearing.

As Corrin was about to compliment Moira, Commander Evrii interrupted their moment.

"Corrin, glad to see you finally awoke and joined the living," she said judgmentally.

Moira glared at Evrii. Evrii was in her armor, towering over Corrin, Grater, and Moira on her Vasari.

Corrin laughed.

"I needed my rest, Commander. You must know how important it is for a leader to be sharp and aware."

Evrii snapped back.

"Yes, I do. But what does the son of The All Father know about leadership and responsibility?"

Grater's eyes widened while Moira clenched her fists.

Corrin again laughed, brushing off Evrii's insult.

"Why doesn't the commander take the day to indulge me in her knowledge of everything she knows?" Corrin said, with a hint of flirtation in his voice.

Evrii's eyes glistened and she smirked. A guard brought Corrin a Vasari. As he mounted it, Evrii took off on hers.

"Try to keep up," she yelled. "The Vasari is the most revered animal on Rashalon. And the fastest!"

Corrin laughed and took off after her.

Behind him Grater yelled, "What about us?!"

"I'll see you at the Gala tonight," Corrin yelled back.

Grater threw his hands up in the air.

"We are from The Black Palace. Corrin is the son of The All Father. How dare she talk to him that way?!" said Moira to Grater, as she angrily stared at Evrii and Corrin riding off together.

Corrin sped after Evrii on his Vasari. The creature was quick and almost felt like it was one with the wind. Its four legs grazed the dirt below. It's long, strong tail whipped behind it. Evrii zoomed through the streets, leading Corrin outside the city and into the plains of Rashalon.

They rode through the marshes and over the hills, leaving civilization behind them. Corrin chased her through the forest and through streams, making his garments wet.

Native animals ran alongside their Vasaris, trying to keep up with their speed. In the distance a herd of wild Vasaris nested along Rashalons untouched land. Corrin was amazed at how beautiful the planet was.

"Can the son of the Father not keep up?" Evrii yelled from up ahead.

Her Vasari was tearing through the dirt. Corrin laughed and made his Vasari ride faster, catching up to Evrii. They rode side by side, catching a glimpse of each other's eyes before nearing a ridge and slowing down.

At the edge, Evrii got off her Vasari and stared at the horizon. Below the ridge was an ocean that spread for miles. Her hair was blowing in the wind as Corrin walked up.

He felt a sense of peace and happiness he hadn't felt in years.

"Rashalon is amazing," he said in awe.

Sea creatures below them were breaking the surface of the water and submerging once again.

"The Shepherd of Fire enjoys tranquility. Who would have thought" Evrii said with a scoff.

Corrin lowered his head, as the breeze swayed his hair and garments.

"Please don't call me that," Corrin said with an embarrassed and shy tone to his voice.

Evrii looked at him and could see that the title Shepherd of Fire was distasteful to Corrin.

She turned to him. "That's your title, isn't it? It's the name you use in battle to congratulate your 'massive victories,'" Evrii said, ending her statement with an annoyed and disgusted look.

Corrin closed his eyes and clenched his jaw. "Given! That title was given to me. I never wanted it," he said, walking away.

Evrii swallowed and continued, even though she noticed how confused Corrin was.

"We never get what we want. Our actions define us and your actions have earned you a name that rings terror across the universe," she bluntly said, anger filling her voice.

Corrin turned around to yell at her but was shocked to see a giant feral beast standing behind Evrii. *"Evrii, look out!"*

As Evrii turned, the beast launched its claws at her. She rolled out the way and whistled for her Vasari.

Corrin reached for his sword and remembered that he had left it back in his guest chamber.

The feral beast roared, dropping down to all fours, and rushed toward Corrin. Evrii mounted her Vasari as Corrin evaded the beast. He jumped and dodged as the beast swung its heavy claws at him.

Evrii rode up, using a baton strapped to her Vasari's saddle to ward the beast off. The beast let out a mighty roar, startling Evrii's Vasari and making it launch her off.

As her Vasari ran away, Corrin sprinted to Evrii's aid as the beast was about to smash down on her. He spun and channeled the energy of the Spears inside him, blasting the beast in the stomach, knocking it down on its back.

As the energy from his hands faded away, he knelt beside Evrii, checking to see if she was injured.

"Are you alright?" he frantically said, searching for any cuts or wounds.

They both were breathing heavily. Looking deep into each other's eyes calmed them. Their faces inched closer together before the defeated beast exerted a painful moan.

Corrin and Evrii looked at the beast, then at each other, before Corrin helped her to her feet. They cautiously walked over and saw that the beast was dying. It was in pain from Corrin's blast and the misery of its slow death was saddening to hear.

Corrin knelt down beside it and placed his hands on its back, rubbing it slowly. Evrii watched in reverence at how Corrin caressed the beast's last moments of life.

"Go now and be with the stars," Corrin whispered into the ear of the beast.

The beast expired after a few more short breaths. Corrin stood up and walked back to his Vasari. Evrii stayed cemented in the same spot, taking in what she had just seen.

After a second of contextualizing what she had just witnessed, she ran up to Corrin.

"What was that?" she frantically asked.

She was confused about what Corrin had just done. Horns in the distance from the city began to blare.

Evrii looked in its direction and then back at Corrin.

"The Gala is starting soon," she said.

Corrin began to mount his Vasari, but Evrii stopped him, demanding answers. "What was that? Why, how, did you do that?"

Corrin smirked and mounted his Vasari, extending his hand.

"Our actions define us," he said, quoting what Evrii had said to him earlier.

Evrii's thoughts and opinions on Corrin began to change after he said that. The stories and rumors of what she'd heard of him were set aside. She grabbed his hand and he mounted her on his Vasari. She wrapped her arms around him, both of them feeling what felt like the start of a new love, as they rode back to the city for the Gala.

CHAPTER 5

OUR ACTIONS DEFINE US

Back in the city, nighttime fell over Rashalon as high society guests from Rashalon and surrounding planets began making their way to the Viceroy Gala.

Street performers put on shows for children and commoners outside the Viceroy Palace. Black Palace troops and Rashalon security guards were stationed all around the city in case of any altercations or disturbances.

All of Rashalon was celebrating tonight's gala, out of tradition for a new leader being elected or because Tirus exemplified a coming change.

Corrin readied himself for the Gala in his guest chambers. His mind was filled with the events of the day and ran with thoughts of possibly having a future with Evrii.

He made his way to the Gala in formal Black Palace attire. His hair brushed against gold shoulder epaulets that connected to a long cape that dragged behind him. His upper body was dressed in black chain mail with cloth material having the insignia of The Black Palace stitched into it. His lower body was covered from waist to toe in the same black chain mail material. He had his sword strapped to his side. Wards bowed to him as he passed them.

As the son of The All Father, everyone was being more formal toward him because of the occasion. Grater and Moira were waiting for him at the entrance of the Gala. They both had formal Black Palace attire on to signify who they were and their status amongst the other guests.

High society guests eyed Corrin, Moira, and Grater as they entered. Whispers rippled throughout the halls, all of them talking about Corrin, his handsomeness, the rumors about his battle victories, and who he was.

"All the wannabes are here tonight, eh?" muffled Grater to Moira and Corrin.

Corrin looked around as all the eyes were on him. Most cut their eyes when he caught them staring, others were bold enough to keep staring and whispering.

"Let's just survive this night, shall we?" Corrin said, taking a deep breath and giving out fake smiles to those who passed him.

Moira rolled her eyes and jolted Corrin and Grater. "You both are children. I grew up going to these kinds of events. It's simple—wave, smile, keep conversations short, and move on. The more you walk and talk, the less people will be bold enough to come up to you. Watch."

Moira grabbed a drink from one the waiter trays and walked to a random group of guests talking. She joined in their conversation. Laughed with them. Took a sip of her drink and then walked away.

As she walked past Corrin and Grater, she smirked. "See. Easy."

She left them to fend for themselves. Corrin and Grater looked at each other with wide eyes. Their moment of awkwardness was cut short by a man who came up and introduced himself to Corrin.

"If it isn't the great Shepherd of Fire," he said, bowing his head. "Corrin, Son of Helena, may she rest in the stars. Son of The All Father, our creator, may he reign for ten thousand cycles," he continued.

Grater rolled his eyes at the sound of this man sounding like an absolute fanatic.

"I am Functionary Jahgros, ranking member of the Rasho council, and proud citizen of the empire."

Jahgros smiled at Corrin, who sensed a strange and pretentious vibe from Jahgros. Jahgros kept smiling as Corrin tried to read him.

Corrin finally answered him back, "Pleasure to meet you, Jahgros. Rashalon is a profound planet with extraordinary citizens," Corrin said, his last word fading off as Evrii walked into the Gala.

Corrin was dumbfounded at how elegant and beautiful she looked. She was wearing a skintight green dress that complimented her body. Her long hair sat on her right shoulder. Her jewelry made her eyes pop. She was the most extravagant person there. Her simple attire was louder than the other guests who were trying too hard to impress other high society members.

"Will you excuse me?" Corrin said, not taking his eyes off Evrii.

Jahgros was left with Grater, who tried to do the fake smile small talk thing Moira had told him about, making Jahgros scoff and walk away.

Corrin pushed through guests and bumped through waiters to reach Evrii as she entered the Gala.

"Commander," he said.

Evrii turned to him, a smile forming on her face as she looked him up and down, admiring and impressed by his outfit.

"Corrin," she said, extending her hand. Corrin grabbed it and gave it a kiss.

"You clean up well," she continued.

"I would say the same to you, but by the looks of it, you don't need my compliments," Corrin responded.

Evrii blushed slightly.

Guests around them began to notice the tension between Corrin and Evrii, embarrassing her.

"Enjoy the night, Corrin," she said, walking off.

"Wait," Corrin said, trying to walk after her but being stopped by guests applauding.

Corrin watched Evrii disappear into the sea of guests before looking at the entrance of the Gala. The guests were applauding as Tirus entered.

As Tirus walked down the stairs into the center of the Gala, guests were congratulating him, bowing, and cheering for his appointment as viceroy. In the distance, Functionary Jahgros was applauding as well, but his eyes told a story of envy and hate, rather than of joy and respect.

After entertaining guests with their admiration and applause, Tirus made his way to Corrin. Tirus gave Corrin a slight bow, out of respect for being the guest of honor.

"None of that Tirus," Corrin said. He extended his hand. "Congratulations, Viceroy," he continued.

Tirus let out a smile and shook his hand. "Thank you, Corrin. Today will be the beginning of a new era," Tirus said. His smile was cut short as Functionary Jahgros approached.

"Viceroy," Jahgros said enthusiastically, giving Tirus a hug and a kiss on both cheeks.

"Jahgros," Tirus greeted back, his voice layered with a stern tone.

"Ah, I see you've met the guest of honor, our great shepherd, Corrin," Jahgros said.

"We met yesterday, Jahgros," Tirus said, giving Jahgros a serious smile.

Jahgros shifted his body, his faux enthusiasm of Tirus being viceroy wavering.

"Oh, you met in private? Without the council members present?" Jahgros inquired, his enthusiasm officially gone.

"You mean without the vultures, and yourself, present?"

Jahgros tried to respond but Tirus cut him off.

"Need I remind you, Jahgros, that affairs of the viceroy, which I was elected as by the people of Rashalon, are not governed or overseen by your council!"

Jahgros clenched his jaw at how sharp Tirus was being with him. He looked at Corrin, and then at Tirus again, before storming off.

Corrin was intrigued at how that interaction went down, making him take more of a liking to Tirus now.

"What was that about?" Corrin asked, as he and Tirus began walking.

"Ah, nothing. Just politics and heat boiling over from the campaign," Tirus responded, waving at guests as he and Corrin strolled through the Gala.

"It seems more than just that, Tirus," Corrin continued.

"Jahgros ran against me for viceroy. He comes from a very rich and powerful family. One of Rashalon's ancient houses. He thinks since he was born into nobility that it's his birthright to rule over our people. He sees someone like me, who came from nothing, as a stain to Rashalon's glory. Politics. Prejudice. Annoyance, I might say."

Corrin heard the stress in Tirus's voice.

"Is he a threat?" Corrin asked, concerned.

"Oh yes, they all are. It comes with the job."

Across the Gala, Corrin spotted Evrii again.

"Excuse me, Viceroy," Corrin said, leaving Tirus to entertain some guests.

Tirus watched as Corrin made his way to Evrii in a hurry.

"You're a hard woman to keep up with," Corrin jokingly said, catching Evrii off guard.

She turned to him, the noise of the Gala drowning out as the two locked gazes once again.

"Only hard if a man can't keep up," she replied, giving Corrin a flirtatious smile.

They walked through the Gala, eyes were on them once again.

"You know, I hate these sorts of events. The pomp, the eyes, the audacious attempt to seem civil," Corrin exclaimed.

Evrii laughed.

"Does Corrin of The Black Palace fear deep pockets and politicians more than the battlefield?" she poked at him.

"I fear not being myself around people who aren't what they say they are," he said, looking her in the eyes.

Evrii was stuck for a moment, before continuing. "You must know a lot about not being who you are," she said, taking a sip of her drink.

"What does that mean, exactly?" Corrin asked, grabbing her arm and stopping her.

Evrii looked at Corrin's hand around her arm, then back at his face.

"You are rumored to be a merciless killer. A brute like your Father. But yet you show compassion to a beast and send it off to the stars in one last act of peace before it dies. You confuse me, Corrin. Or maybe it's you who are confused with yourself! Now, get your hand off me if you ever want it back."

Corrin gulped and slowly released her arm. Her words stabbed him harder than any blade ever could. The tension between them broke the drowning out of the guests as Tirus began making a toast from the center of the Gala.

Guests quieted down as Tirus spoke.

"Proud citizens of Rashalon, guests from surrounding worlds, honored visitors, thank you for joining me today on this beautiful and honorable night as we usher in a new era for this planet."

All the guests were listening to Tirus while Corrin could only hear Evrii's words in his head. The speech Tirus was giving was muffled by Corrin's thoughts and by the conflicting battle that was going on inside him between who he was and who he wanted to be.

THE OLD UNIVERSE

He looked to his side to see Evrii was gone. As he looked forward, he saw her walking up to Tirus and the noise of his inner thoughts faded away.

"…and I wouldn't be here without my gracious and formidable commander by my side. My daughter, Evrii."

Corrin was dumbfounded by hearing that Evrii was Tirus's daughter and let out a scoffing laugh as applause ruptured throughout the Gala.

Evrii smiled and waved to the crowd, making eye contact with Corrin, who was applauding as well. She cut her eyes away quickly and kept smiling and waving.

"And now I would like to let our guest of honor say a few words," Tirus said, nodding toward Corrin.

The gesture caught Corrin by surprise as every pair of eyes turned toward him.

"We are honored and humbled to have Corrin, Son of Helena, Son of The All Father, here in our presence tonight," Tirus continued.

Corrin didn't know what to say. He was never given the opportunity by his Father to speak at events or meetings. He felt that same nervous sweat trickling down his ear before opening his mouth to speak.

"I, uh, thank you, Viceroy Tirus, for indulging me with such taste and reverence," Corrin started, looking around. "I was not prepared to speak so I'll make this short in order for you fine individuals to get back to your gossip," Corrin said, laughing but being serious.

Genuine laughter at his joke danced around the room. Evrii was impressed.

"Songs and tales spread like wildfire across our universe about men and women. Always making the individual a mythical icon rather than a person. Knowing Tirus for a short time, I know he will be one of those people. His love for his world will travel far and wide, immortalizing him as a champion for the people of Rashalon. His actions," Corrin said, looking at Evrii, "will define him. And what he does today, and from here on out, will define him as the man he wants to be, and was meant to be."

Corrin still had his eyes on Evrii as he finished his speech. Thunderous applause rang throughout the Gala.

Evrii and Corrin kept their gazes locked on each other. She couldn't move. Corrin kept his gaze locked on her before being disrupted by Grater.

As Grater began speaking to Corrin, Evrii disappeared out the Gala.

"Fantastic speech. Little dramatic and theatrical for me, but to each their own, eh?"

Corrin's glance followed Evrii as she slipped out back.

"Grater, go…somewhere," Corrin said, his body following his eyes after Evrii.

Grater stood there in disbelief, as Corrin left him alone, again. He mumbled to himself before catching a glimpse of a beautiful woman walking by and went after her.

As Corrin chased after Evrii, Tirus watched from afar, wondering but already knowing what was going on.

Outside the Gala, the moon of Rashalon glimmered down on the planet. Guests were scattered on the balcony, speaking to each other and enjoying the night.

Evrii stood at the end of the balcony looking out toward the fields of her home. Corrin walked over and joined her in taking in the peacefulness of the dark.

"Daughter of the viceroy, and commander," Corrin said, looking at the miles of valley below them.

Evrii playfully rolled her eyes.

"Look, I didn't tell you because—" Evrii started.

"Because you didn't want to be treated differently," Corrin said, cutting her off.

"You must think I'm a hypocrite for how I treated you."

Corrin laughed. "No, quite the opposite," he said.

Evrii turned toward him, shocked to hear him say that.

"You had the opportunity to build something for yourself without your father's shadow looming over you.

You introduced yourself as a fearless commander. A warrior for your people. An intelligent, bright, and beautiful woman," Corrin said, turning his head toward Evrii.

Her heart was racing. "You speak too kindly of me, I…"

Corrin gently put his hand on Evrii's shoulder.

"Shh," he said. "Your actions define you. Now let mine define me."

He leaned in and kissed her, and she kissed him back.

Sunlight forced its way through the drapes and onto Corrin's chest. His attire from the Gala was on the floor next to Evrii's. He turned toward her as some rays from the sun eagerly pushed through the drapes and rested on her sleeping face.

He didn't want to wake her but had to make his way to his ship because he was returning home. He left her a note depicting the little time they had shared together and what it meant to him.

Exiting her room quietly, he made his way to the ship where Grater, Moira, and the rest of the guards waited.

"Your things have been gathered and the crew is ready to take us home," a guard said as Corrin entered the ship.

"Long night?" Grater said, smirking as Corrin took his seat.

Moira angrily glared at Corrin as he was about to answer Grater but smiled instead.

"To The Black Palace," Corrin said.

The ship lifted off and zoomed out of the atmosphere.

From her window, Evrii watched as Corrin left to return to his home. Her bedsheets barely covered her body as she watched the man she might have fallen in love with go back to his life.

As she sat back in her bed, she saw the note he left her and opened it. Tears painted her face as she read through it. Her mesmerized trance was broken by her father.

"You're up," Tirus said.

"The commander of Rashalon's security forces is always up this early," Evrii said, wiping tears away from her eyes.

Tirus walked over and sat on her bed. "I liked him," Tirus said, looking out the window.

Evrii held back tears.

"Your mother would have liked him as well."

Back at The Black Palace, Corrin immediately went to his Father's chambers upon arrival to speak to him about his trip. As he entered The All Father's chambers, the military council and advisors were leaving. Dyerian walked past Corrin as he entered, the two giving each other glaring and dirty looks.

"Ah, my son the diplomat has returned," The All Father said, teasing Corrin.

His towering presence reminded Corrin that he was back in The Black Palace. His long cape dragged behind him as he made his way to his seat.

"Tell me, what news do you bring from Rashalon?" The All Father asked, as he sat. "Is this Tirus the idealist they claim him to be?"

Corrin was taken aback by the "they" in his Father's question.

"They?" Corrin asked. "You mean that little man named Jahgros?"

The All Father glared at Corrin.

"Does he work for you, Father?" Corrin asked, pressing on.

"Corrin, mind yourself. My dealings on my worlds are for me to know and for you to know if I wish it."

Corrin began to get a sense that there was a hidden alliance between his Father and Jahgros but didn't think that much into it.

"The alliance between The Black Palace and Rashalon remains intact. The new viceroy wishes to continue the peace between our worlds. And wishes to proceed forward as a vital member of the empire. He only has one demand that—"

The All Father laughed out loud, cutting Corrin off.

"He has a demand for me?" The All Father continued laughing before seeing that Corrin was being serious.

"What 'demand' does this creature have for his creator?" The All Father asked chillingly, all sorts of laughter diminishing in the air.

Corrin spoke frankly, "The new viceroy demands the end of all Rasho boys being conscripted into your armies."

The All Father clenched his fist.

"I should have you beaten for bringing such idiotic demands to me," The All Father said, glaring at Corrin.

Corrin tightened up.

"You think you are a diplomat now. So, tell me, my son, shall I destroy Rashalon for this disrespect? Shall I drain its oceans, starve its people, pillage its homes, and take its women for the contempt its leader has shown me and my grace?"

The All Father stood up and raised his hand, calling for the Spear of Space, which came zooming from the top of The Black Palace and into his grasp.

All Corrin could think of was the danger he might have put Evrii in.

The All Father circled Corrin, looking him up and down. "Or shall I entertain this viceroy and his demands? Lending my mercy in exchange for praise and gratitude for being a generous God!"

The All Father made his way back to his seat and sat down. Corrin rapidly organized his thoughts and chose his next words carefully.

"You've defeated all your enemies. Pugart is in ashes. The known worlds of this universe are in your command. The empire, your planetary kingdom, will forever be in your mercy. And now, Father, that we have entered into a time of peace, the need for a growing army, an army that serves you, is no longer needed. You have enough soldiers to carry out your orders. Show Rashalon how great The All Father who yields the Spear of Space truly is. Grant this viceroy his petty wish."

Corrin hyped his Father up as much as possible in hopes to calm any idea he had of laying waste to Rashalon.

The All Father pondered Corrin's words. "Yes," he said.

Corrin let out a sigh.

"Peace is upon us. I have united this universe under one banner. Send word to Rashalon—tell this new viceroy that The All Father has ended the conscription of Rasho boys into his army."

The All Father, for the first time in a while, looked at peace. Corrin sensed a new era coming.

"Father, if you don't mind, I would like to deliver the news personally," Corrin said.

He stuttered as he continued, "I-I believe news like this coming directly from myself on your command would show the viceroy the magnitude of your generosity."

"Go, my son. Deliver this extension of my grace."

Corrin bowed to his Father and began to leave.

"And say hello to her for me."

Corrin stopped in his tracks, his eyes wide. He turned around.

"I have eyes and ears everywhere, son."

Corrin didn't know what to say.

"I don't speak much about your mother. Sometimes I feel unworthy to even speak her name."

Corrin couldn't even remember the last time he had heard his Father bring up his mother.

"I have never known another woman like her. And I have never felt again what she made me feel."

Corrin tried to speak, "Father, I—" but The All Father cut him off.

"Silence. Go to Rashalon. Deliver my message to the viceroy. Have fun with this Rasho girl. Enjoy yourself. Let love consume you. Embrace it. Then destroy it. The Black Palace has many suitable women here for you to take, plant your seed in, and continue my bloodline. Understood, Corrin?"

Corrin gulped and clenched his jaw.

"Yes, Father, I do."

But Corrin lied to his Father that day. He didn't understand. He went back to Rashalon and informed Viceroy Tirus about his Father's decision to end the conscription of Rasho boys into the armies of The All Father.

Corrin was praised by Tirus and all of Rashalon for brokering this deal with the creator. As time went by, Corrin stayed on Rashalon while peace reigned over the universe.

He did indeed listen to his Father and allowed himself to be consumed by love for Evrii. They both embraced it and spent months together on Rashalon building an unbreakable relationship.

Instead of destroying it like his Father had advised, Corrin eventually asked for Evrii's hand in marriage. The All Father was furious at first but submitted to Corrin's love for Evrii.

At their wedding, The All Father announced that Corrin was now leader of all the worlds, anointing him with the title Lord Corrin.

He gave Corrin and Evrii Arcadia, a planet he had created after the death of Helena. A planet sacred to him and pieced together by the Spear of Space.

Untouchable by any power, outside destruction, and even the Spear itself, Arcadia was the most beautiful planet ever seen in the universe. Corrin and Evrii began a life there. Arcadia became a beacon of change throughout the universe. People from all planets moved there and began anew.

During this time of peace Corrin began reading again, diving into all the various cultures under his Father's rule. He formed and trained an elite guard on Arcadia who were called the warrior priests. These warrior priests trained and studied in the cosmic arts under Corrin and eventually became teachers to Lord Corrin and Evrii's children, Kale and Lynn.

Peace reigned over the universe for what was called the Twelve Good Years before destiny shattered it all.

CHAPTER 6

NEW WORLDS

Yelling woke Corrin up from a deep sleep. He had gone to the outskirts of Arcadia the night before with his son, Kale, and his most trusted warrior priest, Zhao-Lan, to watch the planetary eclipse of Vaxlier behind the sun of Arcadia.

Vaxlier was a lava planet with one landmass. The fountains of Vaxlier were pillars of ancient blacksmiths standing tall with their crafted legs deep into the planet's core, allowing the hottest lava to pour through the statues. Some of the strongest weapons in the universe were forged there.

Corrin made it a tradition on Arcadia to take his son every year to watch the planetary eclipse.

It's been twelve long and peaceful years since his last battle. His hands were now rugged from writing, farming, and hunting.

As he rose from his bed, his different-colored eyes were blinded by the brightness of the sun hitting his face. His hair fell to the middle of his back as he scratched his thick beard. The yelling that woke him up made its way to his bedchamber as his daughter, Lynn, came running in.

"Father, tell Kale to stop messing with my potions! He's going to mess up my presentation to Zhao-Lan!"

Lynn was nine years old and skilled with potions and alchemy. These forms of spear-energy-channeling originated from the Zordic Clans of Wa-Rin and were studied by Corrin and his warrior priests during the Twelve Good Years.

"Zhao-Lan said I have to master this next test in order to move on to learning how to channel the energy of the spears within me," Lynn exclaimed, pouting and jumping onto Corrin's bed.

Kale walked in and leaned against the door. He was a spitting image of Corrin. Turning thirteen soon, he was training just as hard as his father had at that age, focusing more on learning how to use various styles of blades across the universe. His skill in channeling spear energy though was nowhere near as potent as his younger sister.

Corrin rubbed Lynn's dark brown hair. She had her mother's light purple eyes and glared at her brother who was trying not to laugh.

"Kale," Corrin said, holding back a deep yawn. "Give your sister back her potions and make sure your armor is cleaned for your lesson today with Van-Mer," Corrin said.

"But Dad—" Kale started to protest.

"Ah," Corrin cut him off. "Go!"

Kale sighed and stormed off.

Lynn smiled and gave Corrin a kiss on the cheek and ran off after Kale. Their clamoring could be heard down the hall as Evrii walked into the room, looking back and laughing at them.

"I see those two finally got you out of bed," she said.

Corrin laughed and fell back onto his pillows.

"What are you talking about? I'm still in here. Join me," he said back to her jokingly.

Evrii put down a basket she was carrying, making sure the kids were gone, as her smile faded away. Corrin noticed how serious she got and sat up in bed.

"What did I do now? Whatever it is I'll make it up to you," he said flirtatiously, reaching toward Evrii.

"Dyerian is here," she said, her face and tone painted with worry.

Corrin's demeanor quickly became serious.

"Here? Now? Where?!"

He got out of bed quickly and dressed himself.

"He's in your study."

Corrin gave her an "are you serious?" look as he tied his robe.

"I don't like this, Corrin. What does he want?" Evrii asked nervously.

Corrin left the room without answering, more nervous than his wife. He entered into his study cautiously, not knowing what Dyerian wanted or why he had come to Arcadia unannounced.

As he entered the room, Dyerian was standing around, looking in disgust at the countless books, art, artifacts, and technology from various worlds and cultures Corrin had gathered. Dyerian wasn't alone though. Grater stood by the window of the study.

After Rashalon, when peace reigned over the universe for the Twelve Good Years and when Corrin became Lord of the worlds, Grater continued his path under The All Father's shadow.

He rose quickly in the ranks, next to Dyerian, who was now close to becoming a general in the All Father's military. Corrin proposed Grater for the position, but Dyerian's brute will and callous respect for life made him a better choice to lead thought The All Father. Now Grater was basically Dyerian's errand boy.

"Corrin, it's been a while," Grater said, walking over and giving Corrin a hug.

Corrin was happy to see his best friend. He hugged him back, missing the times they had spent together.

"It's good to see you, Grater."

Grater was going to speak but Dyerian cut him off.

"Lieutenant, wait outside," Dyerian said sternly, keeping his glare locked on Corrin.

Grater looked at Corrin, then back at Dyerian and nodded, exiting the room and closing the door behind him. Corrin didn't like how Dyerian treated Grater and his soldiers. He had heard rumors and stories about how merciless he was with the troops under his command.

"You look tired, Dyerian. Has my Father treated you well?" Corrin said, taking a jab at Dyerian being a sheep for whatever The All Father wanted.

"I'm sure my life has been more meaningful and well-off than yours. You locking yourself in this museum you call a home while the universe expands," Dyerian said, picking up a book from Corrin's table and placing it back down.

Corrin scratched his beard and laughed. "If you have something to say, Dyerian, say it fast before I embarrass you in front of the men you command!"

Dyerian gripped his blade and took a step toward Corrin but retreated back. Even with all his training, promotion, and brute size, Dyerian was no match for Corrin and deep down he knew it. The two glared at each other for a moment longer before Dyerian gave up and told Corrin why he was there.

"The All Father requests your immediate presence at The Black Palace," Dyerian said through his teeth, wishing he had the strength to kill Corrin where he stood.

"And he sent his errand boy to tell me that? Why am I being summoned?!" Corrin asked, wondering why his Father, after all these years, would summon him to

The Black Palace abruptly, without notice, and with Dyerian as the messenger.

"Ask him yourself," Dyerian said, heading to the door.

Corrin pondered the reason he was being summoned as Dyerian was leaving.

"Dyerian, aren't you forgetting something?" Corrin said with a teasing tone.

With his back to Corrin, Dyerian angrily rolled his eyes and turned to face him. He placed his fist on his chest and bowed his head as he angrily said, "Lord Corrin," and stormed off.

Corrin laughed at making Dyerian squirm.

He watched out the window of his study as Dyerian and his men boarded their ship and left Arcadia's atmosphere. His joyful face of making Dyerian address him as his superior faded as the thoughts of why his Father wanted to see him begin to fill his mind.

He sat down in his study thinking about it heavily before Evrii walked in. She could tell a lot was on his mind and made her way behind him, placing her hands on his shoulders softly.

"What's the matter?" Evrii asked, rubbing Corrin's shoulders.

"I've been summoned to The Black Palace on urgent business," Corrin reluctantly said, reaching back and placing his hand on Evrii's.

She could see how stressed Corrin was and replied with assurance, "Whatever the matter is, you can handle it. You are magnificent, Corrin. A great leader. A great father. Whatever He wants will never change how I and our children see you." Evrii's strong words gave Corrin a sense of peace.

He stood up and faced her. "I love you," he said as they kissed each other.

After Evrii and Corrin spoke in his study, Corrin traveled to The Black Palace to meet with The All Father. The last time he was there was years ago when the official word of peace across the universe was put into effect.

Wards looked at Corrin in awe as he made his way to his Father's chambers. The young man they knew was no more and what they saw was a new, confident, self-aware individual who formed his own destiny outside the wishes of his Father's.

The Corrin who left to Rashalon twelve years ago was a shadow of who Corrin had grown to be.

Whispers rippled through and bounced off Corrin like never before. Usually, the weight of eyes and low talk would make Corrin nervous, but older and more assured now of who he is, the things that would have bothered him in the past no longer fazed him. As he reached his Father's chambers, he heard men inside chattering and The All Father yelling at them.

Corrin opened the massive chamber doors and walked in, seeing The All Father sitting at the head of a long table. His room had changed from the last time Corrin had seen it. The bed was gone. Decorations had been removed. The chamber now looked like a military room with maps, schematics of weapons, and a hologram of the entire planetary kingdom in the center of the table.

Generals of The All Father's forces were there as well but were getting up to leave as Corrin made his way inside. Some of them bowed their heads and murmured, "Lord Corrin" as they passed him, others cut their eyes away.

Dyerian was there as well and left the room with the other generals, passing by Corrin and giving him another look of disgust, making Corrin laugh to himself.

As Corrin got closer to the table, he saw the hologram outline of the planetary kingdom was enormous and detailed. He knew the empire was gigantic but was seeing for the first time in one place how expansive the kingdom was that his Father built.

The All Father was sitting in his chair at the head of table, his hand on his head. He looked stressed but still powerful. His dark blue skin and deep white eyes seemed to lighten up at the sight of Corrin.

"My son," he said, motioning Corrin to have a seat.

"I give you Arcadia, make you Lord of All, and you can't even pay me a visit every once in a while?" he pouted, standing up and pressing a button to make the hologram outlining of the planetary kingdom go away.

Corrin felt bad for not coming to see his Father on occasion and responded, "Forgive me, Father. Shaping Arcadia into a place of solidarity and peace for its citizens, immigrants, and my children has been my main focus. I am in debt to you for allowing me to focus on a future for my new home."

The All Father looked at Corrin for a moment, already getting a sense that the son he had raised was a mere memory in the shadow of who Corrin now was. But that didn't stop him from moving forward with why he had summoned Corrin to The Black Palace.

"In my debt you say?" The All Father said, folding his hands on his lap. "A debt you can now repay!"

Corrin shifted in his seat, not knowing what his Father meant and worried to find out.

The All Father stood up from his seat and motioned his hand over the table. Corrin watched as the hologram outline of the planetary kingdom reappeared.

"What do you see?" asked The All Father, glaring into the hologram.

"The worlds under your control," Corrin said.

"The 'known' worlds," The All Father said, placing his hands on the table and leaning in.

Corrin looked at him. He could see something he hadn't seen in his Father in years. Determination.

"While you were busy in Arcadia building a place of 'solidarity and peace,' like you said, for the future of your new home. I was busy focusing on my future!"

Corrin could hear a sinister tone in his Father's voice.

The All Father put his hand over the hologram and swiped again. As he was swiping, Corrin saw the cosmos and places in the universe he had never seen before. He stood up slowly as The All Father kept swiping.

Miles and miles of stars sped through Corrin's eyes before a small planet appeared. Surrounding it was two moons.

The All Father swiped again and another planet appeared. A giant planet with a ring of asteroids around it and four moons orbiting it.

The All Father kept swiping and more planets Corrin had never seen appeared on the hologram.

"Father, what is this?" Corrin whispered, concerned with what he was seeing.

The All Father walked back to his seat and sat down. Corrin still stood, looking at the last planet The All Father swiped on.

"It's the next step in my expansion. Our expansion!"

Corrin quickly looked at his Father.

"Expansion?!"

"During these twelve years of peace, as my worlds reaped the harvest I gave them, I set my eyes out farther into the vast universe the Spears of Time and Space created."

Corrin was still standing. He couldn't bring himself to sit down or even move.

"The Spear of Space neglected to inform me that new worlds had been created. Worlds out in space not knowing that I am here to set them on a righteous path of guidance and obedience."

Corrin was shocked to hear what his Father was saying. He thought the planetary kingdom, peace, and the current grip of power his Father had on the worlds was enough.

"It's time these worlds know their place in my universe and know who their God is!"

Corrin kept his eyes on his Father, looked back at the hologram, and then back at his Father.

"You're planning to conquer these worlds," Corrin uttered.

The All Father scoffed, "Conquer. Such a barbarian word. Assimilation is more like it. Can you see, Corrin?"

The All Father stood and started walking to Corrin. "The universe, these new planets."

The All Father reached Corrin and placed his heavy blue hands on Corrin's shoulders.

"They all will belong to you in time. To your son. To his sons and so forth."

Corrin wanted to denounce this. He wanted to yell and tell his Father what he was doing was wrong. He thought he had outgrown the grip his Father had over him. But he couldn't bring himself to object.

"You shouldn't send your men to invade these planets we know nothing about," Corrin said, not making eye contact with his Father who was towering over him.

What he really meant was that his Father shouldn't send anyone to these planets. But The All Father manipulated Corrin's words.

"Of course not," The All Father said, walking back to his chair and sitting down.

"That's why I am sending you."

Corrin looked up, confused.

"I trust you to open up a dialogue with these new worlds. Introduce them to a higher purpose—me. Allow them to willingly submit to my empire."

Corrin was going to speak, but The All Father cut him off.

"You can convince these worlds without any blood being shed. Six new worlds filled with beings, resources, culture, and identity. Something you love, right?"

The All Father was messing with Corrin's head, using strong manipulation and conniving tactics on him to make him agree.

Corrin pondered it all.

"No war. No use of force. No invasions if they decline to submit," Corrin said, finally laying out demands and speaking with the confidence he had built for the past twelve years.

The All Father smiled. "You are the Lord of my worlds, and will be the Lord of these worlds, if they choose to submit."

"And if they don't submit?" Corrin asked, with a little more power behind his voice. The faces of Hivli, the people of Halvodon, and the rebels on Pugart quickly flashed in his mind.

"Then we let them be as they are," The All Father responded.

Corrin was relieved to hear this but still had reservations.

"Will you grant me a few days to think and reflect on this before agreeing to join you?" Corrin asked.

He expected his Father to immediately yell and get angry at him even asking such a question, but The All Father agreed.

"Sleep on it. Speak it over with whom you seek counsel these days."

Back on Arcadia that evening, as nighttime began to lay a deep blanket of stars and darkness over the planet, Corrin told Evrii what the meeting with The All Father was about. She listened in silence to it all and didn't speak a word until Corrin was done. She stood up and walked around their bedchamber, thinking.

"I don't know what to do," Corrin said.

She stopped in her tracks and looked at him and then kept walking around.

"Evrii, say something," Corrin pleaded.

"What do you want me to say?" she blurted out. "It seems like you have already decided!"

Corrin sank into the couch he was sitting on.

"You gave up the life your Father molded for you to be here, with me and our children. To build a world for ourselves. For all people. And now you're being dragged right back into his grasp."

Corrin protested, "He offered me a role. I can choose to decline if I want to."

Evrii laughed and shook her head. "You really think you have a choice? Look at you, you know he won't let you just lead an 'introductory' mission to these new planets!"

Corrin sat silently.

Evrii composed herself and walked over to Corrin. She sat beside him, placed her hand on his leg, and moved his hair out of his face with her other hand.

"My love, those worlds, those people, who have lived without knowing your Father's rule, deserve to continue their existence without ever being in tune with what the worlds under his control have had to endure."

Corrin sighed and looked at her. She could tell he was once again fighting an internal battle between being his own man, and the man his Father wanted him to be.

"I'll go to him tomorrow and tell him I want no part in this."

Evrii gave him a smile of relief.

She placed her hands on his face and then hugged him. While her head lay on his chest, Corrin couldn't shake off the feeling of something not being right.

CHAPTER 7

THE DIVISION

The glowing rays of Arcadia's moon filtered into Corrin's room and danced on Evrii's face as she slept. Corrin lay beside her, twisting and turning in his sleep. His dreams were once again filled with the faces of those he had sent to the grave.

As the faces consumed his dreams, he woke up abruptly. His hair was sticking to his back and face as his body was drenched with sweat. Evrii still slept peacefully as Corrin slid out of bed and walked to the balcony of the room.

He looked beyond Arcadia's landscape while the people below him slept in their homes. He looked up to the night sky and wondered why the visions he had twelve years ago were now coming back. He hadn't seen those images in his head for years. He thought they were just skirmishes of time and his body fighting his inner consciousness. But the visions this time felt so vivid and real to him.

He looked back at Evrii who was still sleeping inside. The eerie feel of something horrible coming draped itself over Corrin and consumed him. He thought about the meeting from earlier and went to his study to go over the schematics.

In his study, Arcadia's moon glimmered through the windows as he looked over the schematics. He couldn't help but think there was something his Father wasn't telling him. The schematics had the coordinates and locations of the new worlds and Corrin readied himself silently to go there. Something inside him told him to go. He didn't know why, but he trusted his gut.

He scurried out of his home and into a clearing outside of Arcadia's capital.

Years of focusing on himself, his family, and his new home allowed Corrin to grow in channeling the cosmic spear energy inside him.

The Ovaseryns had taught him how to channel the energy from the Spear as a young man, but as he got older and trained and studied more, Corrin learned how to channel the energy inside him better than any being. Some ancient beings across the known worlds had even whispered that his expertise might have possibly made him stronger than The All Father himself.

As Corrin entered the clearing, he knelt down and placed his fists on the ground. He took a deep breath and leaped into the air, zooming out of Arcadia's atmosphere and into space.

He zoomed past the nearby planets and beamed toward the new worlds. His speed was immeasurable. He was radiating energy brighter and more blinding than any comet.

A trip that would take any normal being in space about four to six months by ship took Corrin a few minutes with the power of the Spears flowing inside him.

As he reached the first new planet, he floated above its atmosphere. Its orbit was strong and pulled in anything that got too close.

Corrin flew into the atmosphere and descended below the clouds into the world. He landed on the surface and looked around. He expected to hear animals or be greeted by a security team. But nothing happened.

As he looked around some more, he saw smoke coming from over a mountain range. He immediately thought that's where the inhabitants of the world must be stationed or lived.

He leaped into the air again and zoomed toward the mountain range. He wanted to get a closer look but didn't want to draw attention to himself as an outsider or be seen as an invader or threat, so he landed on the mountain and walked over the edge. The mountain was full of snow and Corrin could see vegetation growing.

Near the edge of the mountain he noticed tracks of feet in the snow. They were small, the size of a child. Corrin squatted down and cautiously got closer.

As he did, he saw the body of a child sprawled out. The child was barely dressed and definitely wasn't in the right clothes to be up in a mountain full of cold snow.

Corrin rushed over and turned the child over. It was a small girl. She looked about his daughter's age. Corrin frantically looked around to see if there was any sign of others, but the only tracks he saw was hers leading to where she had collapsed.

Corrin shook her and checked to see if she was breathing. Her arms and legs were badly burned and her clothes smelled of smoke.

As Corrin checked her breathing some more, she opened her eyes slowly and grabbed Corrin's arm, spooking him.

"What happened to you? Are you alone?" Corrin asked, confused and concerned for this child.

"They came from the sky," she said faintly, barely holding on to life.

"They brought fire and death," she muttered.

Corrin had no idea what she was saying.

"Who did?" he asked softly. "Where is your family?" he asked, his thoughts racing.

The girl, weak and on the brink of passing into the next life, raised her arm and pointed toward the smoke coming from the edge of the mountain.

Corrin scooped the girl from the snow and held her in his arms as he walked over to the edge of the mountain.

As he reached the edge, his eyes widened in despair as he saw a city below him consumed in flames and destruction. Miles of ash and decay spread out across the land. Corrin made his way down the ridge with the girl in his arms.

The smell of burning wood filled the air as Corrin weaved through the city streets. He wondered who did this and why.

The only noise was from the cracking of fire and pieces of buildings falling to the ground. A mildly burned carriage full of hay was flipped in front of him and he turned it back on its wheels to place the girl on.

"Where is your family?" he asked. "Where are all the people?"

Before the girl could answer, Corrin got a whiff of a foul smell in the wind. A glimpse of something in the distance caught his eye and as he looked, his mouth dropped. He slowly walked toward it, which led him into the center of the city. Corrin dropped to his knees as tears filled his eyes. He had found the rest of the people.

The foul smell was coming from what remained of their charred and burnt skin. The bodies were piled on top of each other like stacked wood. Corrin gagged at the smell and sight, almost throwing up where he knelt.

He dropped his hands to the ground and held back the vomit, his tears hitting the ground like arrows being released by the strongest archer.

As he slowly lifted his head, he saw in the distance something that looked familiar. He stood up and rushed over, wiping away the tears from his face.

Reaching the familiar object, he picked it up quickly, brushing off the ash and blood. His sadness turned to anger and ferocity as he held in his hands a fragment of Black Palace armor.

He looked around manically, realizing his Father had lied to him. He yelled and pulled his hair at what The All Father had done. Corrin stood in the midst of the destruction and death holding on to the fragment of Black Palace armor.

He looked up to the sky and glared into the atmosphere as if his Father was looking back at him.

Gripping the fragment of armor tight, he remembered the little girl and ran back to her.

Her eyes were closed and Corrin tried waking her up to take her back to Arcadia with him. As he tried waking her, her body was cold and she didn't move.

Corrin's heart skipped a beat as he realized she was dead.

He closed his eyes as rage consumed him. He wanted to fly back to The Black Palace and kill everyone who stopped him from strangling his Father, but he composed himself. He needed to first check if the other planets had been laid to waste like this one. Before leaving, he placed his hand on the girl and whispered, "Go be with the stars now."

Outside the city, Corrin knelt down and zoomed up into the atmosphere, exiting the planet. Hate and anger filled Corrin's body as he beamed to the next world.

As he approached, he saw one of The All Father's carrier ships hovering over the planet. It was an intelligence ship, used to map out strategic landing points from above a world for an invasion plan.

Corrin hovered close to it, wondering if he should warn the planet or enter the ship and try to stop them. Pondering what to do, he decided to enter the ship.

He glided toward it. Soldiers inside recognized him and opened the hatch to let him in. The commanding officer of the ship greeted him with open arms.

"Lord Corrin, we were not expecting you," the commander said, bowing his head.

Corrin was breathing heavily and was unsettled. The commanding officer and soldiers on board could see that Corrin was distraught. The commanding officer noticed the silence and uneasiness in the air and spoke again. "Lord Corrin, can I offer you any food or accommodations? We were not informed about your arrival so excuse my men for—"

Corrin pushed past him and cut him off. "Turn this ship around," he said.

The soldiers looked at the commanding officer, who was shocked and confused.

"My lord, we were stationed here by direct orders of The All Father to gather intelligence. We can't disobey direct orders."

Corrin was getting frantic. "Turn this ship around *now*!" he yelled.

Some of the soldiers began gripping their side blasters and swords.

The commanding officer was taken aback by Corrin's outburst and responded sternly, "We cannot break protocol, my lord!"

Corrin was still gripping the broken fragment of Black Palace armor he had found and noticed the commanding officer and soldiers were now staring at it.

"Why don't I radio to command?" the commanding officer said as he motioned toward an SOS button.

Corrin knew what that meant and reacted quickly.

He kicked one of the soldiers into the other and swung the broken armor fragment, smashing in the glass face mask of another soldier.

The commanding officer leaped at Corrin, trying to bear grab him, but Corrin ducked, sending the officer flying over Corrin's back and into the wall of the ship.

More soldiers came around the corner and Corrin took them on, disabling them from their weapons and knocking them out instead of killing them.

The commanding officer tried rushing Corrin again but Corrin kicked him to the ground and pressed his foot on his neck.

"This ship is leaving, and this world will be spared," Corrin said through his teeth.

As Corrin released the pressure of his foot from the commanding officer's neck, a young soldier was regaining his consciousness from being knocked out.

He saw Corrin stepping on the commanding officer's neck and pulled out his blaster.

As Corrin turned, the soldier shot at him, missing and causing an explosion inside the ship. Corrin rushed to the young soldier and kicked the blaster out of his hand.

The commanding officer stood up quickly and looked at the explosion and then at Corrin. They both knew that the shot from the blaster had hit one of the ship's main pipelines and would lead to the engine, causing an explosion.

Corrin glared at the commanding officer then moved quickly.

"Get your men to the evacuation pods."

The commanding officer stood still, breathing heavily, piercing Corrin with his glare.

"Go!" Corrin yelled.

The commanding officer sucked up his pride and yelled for his men to help the others who were still mildly unconscious to the evacuation pods.

Fire from the explosion rapidly spread across the ship. Corrin tried putting it out, but the fire had already reached the engine. The blast was so sudden and violent that it launched Corrin out into space, exploding into the darkness of the universe.

He regathered himself, his clothes slightly burned. His vision was blurred and his head was pounding as he looked for the escape pod. When he didn't see it, he zoomed closer to the exploded ship.

Large pieces of the ship were falling into the planet's atmosphere while other pieces floated off into the universe. The commanding officer and soldiers hadn't made it off in time.

Corrin grunted.

He didn't want these men to die. He only wanted to stop his Father from invading this planet and causing further havoc. But now Corrin thought that he might have started something irreversible.

He left the wreckage of the ship and beamed back to Arcadia.

Dawn was barely breaking as Corrin landed on his balcony. Evrii was still asleep as he softly walked to her bedside and kissed her on the forehead. He knew this would be the last time anyone he loved and cared about had a peaceful morning.

Gripping the broken fragment of Black Palace armor in his hand still, Corrin leaped into the air and zoomed to The Black Palace.

The sun was beginning to hit the black walls of the fortress as Corrin landed strongly on the ground outside the gates. Guards watched as he stormed inside and up to The All Father's chambers.

A ward came running up to him.

"My lord, the Father is asleep. He must not be distur…"

Corrin pushed the ward aside and continued to his Father's chambers.

He kicked open the chamber doors and walked in.

"Father!" he yelled.

He remembered that his Father's bedchamber no longer had a bed and had been turned into a strategic room for The All Father to have easy and quick access to military plans.

The ward Corrin pushed aside came running in. Corrin turned around and grabbed him by the shirt collar and pulled him in close.

"Where is he?" Corrin whispered.

Corrin followed the ward's eyes that pointed toward the staircase that led to The All Father's throne. Corrin released the ward and headed up the staircase.

As he reached the top, he saw The All Father sleeping. Corrin threw the broken fragment of armor onto the bed.

"Wake up!" Corrin yelled, *"Wake up!"*

The All Father opened his eyes slowly and turned to see Corrin standing in front of the bed.

"What's the meaning of this?" The All Father demanded.

He noticed the fragment of armor on the bed and Corrin's demeanor. Corrin's clothes were still burnt from the explosion. He was breathing heavily and had rage in his eyes. His white eye was glowing rapidly. He was pacing back and forth, shaking his head at what he had discovered.

The All Father glared at him. The Spear of Space rested on its pedestal and was softly radiating, almost as if it was feeding off the tension.

"You lied to me!" Corrin finally said.

The All Father looked at The Black Palace armor fragment and leaned back into his bed. He realized Corrin had gone to the new worlds.

"You lied to yourself!" The All Father responded. "You thought you were going to live a common life of studying and leisure, with a wife and children. Children who have my blood. Everything I have built is for you. And will be for your chil—"

Corrin cut The All Father off for the first time in his life. *"You slaughtered those people. Destroyed that world!"*

Corrin's voice was loud and strong. He no longer had any fear of not speaking his mind to his Father.

The All Father's eyebrows burrowed. His white eyes began glowing. The Spear of Space radiated even more now.

"Watch yourself, Corrin. Just because you are my son, does not mean you can speak to me how you please."

"You lied to me and thought I wouldn't find out. You think I will allow my family, *my* children, to attach their names to *anything* you have built? You are a destroyer!"

The All Father thrust forward, still sitting in bed.

"Watch your tongue, boy!" The All Father said angrily.

Corrin did not care. He continued, "Everything I hate about myself is from you. Everything the people in this universe fears comes from your lust and need for power. You turned me into a killer. A herald for your deeds. My mother would have hated the monster you have become!"

Corrin knew those final words would pierce The All Father.

The All Father lunged at Corrin from his bed and went to slap him, but Corrin stopped his hand and pushed him back into the bed frame, making it crack from the force.

The All Father looked at Corrin in disbelief.

Corrin himself couldn't believe that he had just put his hands on his Father, The All Father, the bearer of the Spear of Space, but he held his composure and didn't ease up.

"I am not afraid of you anymore. You have no command over my life and decisions from here on out. I know who I am and what I have built for myself."

"You are no son of mine," The All Father muttered. "You're a traitor to The Black Palace! I revoke your title of lord! I revoke your lands!"

The All Father was still speaking as Corrin began leaving.

The All Father's voice got louder. "Arcadia is no longer yours! Your command over *my* worlds is no more!"

Before Corrin left, he turned back to his Father.

"You will stop any invasion plans you have commenced. If you go forward with this, I will retaliate," Corrin said solemnly.

The All Father burst from his bed. As he launched into space, he reached for the Spear that zoomed to his hand, covering The All Father immediately in his armor.

The All Father crashed back down to the ground, shaking the very foundation of The Black Palace. His landing sent out gusts of wind that made the walls of The Black Palace tremble. The gusts rippled out into the universe as well, causing quakes on nearby moons.

The All Father pointed the Spear of Space at Corrin. His eyes and the Spear were glowing out of control.

"How dare you command me?!"

Corrin did not budge. He felt the warmth of the Spear's energy getting hotter and hotter until it burned, then nothing. He continued to stare into his Father's deep white eyes, until he turned around to leave.

The All Father couldn't bring himself to kill Corrin on the spot but kept yelling as Corrin left The Black Palace.

"You are weak. You always have been weak. You're a disgrace to my bloodline. You are nothing!"

Corrin and the entire Black Palace could hear The All Father yelling as Corrin made his way out the gates.

He couldn't believe he had just faced his Father, the creator, and lived. For the first time in his life, Corrin felt a sense of danger take over his body. Never in his whole life had he ever had to deal with being in fear of his life, but now, he realized he had just made an enemy he could not fathom. He leaped into the air and zoomed back to Arcadia as the things he just set in motion unfolded.

CHAPTER 8

WE ARE WITH YOU

The Arcadian sun had already illuminated the entire planet as Corrin zoomed into its atmosphere and landed in front of his home.

The weight of having gone completely against his Father dropped him to his knees as the sounds of Arcadian birds flew above him.

The pressure he felt all those years ago as a pawn for his Father's vision rushed into his mind filling him with fear, anxiety, and doubt. He could not bring himself to realize what he had done.

From their balcony, Evrii saw Corrin on his knees in distress and immediately ran to him. Lynn and Kale peered from the door as their mother picked up their battered father and took him inside.

"Kale," Evrii said anxiously but sternly. "Take your sister to your room and don't come out until I say so!"

Kale could see the seriousness in his mother's eyes. He looked down at his father who looked like he had stared into the eyes of death, and took his little sister away.

Evrii scrambled to get rags to clean away the ash and residue on Corrin. He was unresponsive to Evrii's pleas to tell her what had happened.

Everything around Corrin was a blur and moving in slow motion. As wards rushed in and out to help Evrii take off Corrin's burnt clothes, the magnitude of Corrin's battling emotions knocked him out.

Corrin fell into a deep sleep where he had dreams of his childhood. Dreams that told a tale of what he always thought was correct: honor his Father, honor the memory of his mother, become the leader of the universe, and rule as the God his Father wanted him to be.

But his false reality during his dreams was shattered as the visions of death engulfed his mind again. The vision this time seemed darker and more vivid, making him wake up yelling.

His body was drenched in sweat as he looked around and noticed he was in his own bed. The sun of Arcadia was already beginning to set.

He felt an eerie calmness in his room and realized he didn't hear his children or the chattering of wards in the halls. He cautiously hopped out of bed, wrapped himself in one of his robes, and exited his room, seeing the halls empty.

He remembered his Father calling him a traitor and feared that The All Father had already retaliated by coming for his wife and children.

Corrin ran through the halls fast, still weak but determined. He checked Kale's room and saw that it was empty. Fear began biting at him. He bolted to Lynn's room, hoping to find her there with her brother. But her room was empty as well.

"Lynn! Kale! Evrii!" Corrin yelled.

He frantically yelled their names, fearing the worst until Evrii came running around the corner. Corrin looked at her in relief. She ran to him and they embraced each other.

"I thought, I thought…" Corrin started.

He couldn't bring himself to say what he thought had happened to them.

"Where are the children? Where is everyone?" Corrin asked, concerned.

"The children are fine. They are safe with Van-Mer at Leerauh. I didn't want them to see you like this."

Leerauh is a small island in Arcadia where Corrin and his family would go during the summer solstice.

"I sent the wards home. You need to tell us what happened!"

Corrin was at peace knowing his children were away from the city but was confused.

"Us?" he said.

Evrii walked Corrin into the mess hall of their home where Zhao-Lan and some of the warrior priests sat and stood.

At the table sitting with Zhao-Lan were Kan, Wi-Lao, Sun-Tro, Giro-Po, Fae-Zung, and Drisa-Yun. The other warrior priests stood around them, proud to see Corrin on his feet once again.

After Corrin became lord of the universe and took Arcadia as his home, he had recruited the warriors of the planet Wa-Rin to be his guards, teachers, and eventually, friends. They were a loyal band of brothers and sisters who surpassed the formal settings of titles and hierarchy and instead had become a family to Corrin.

Across the room, a dim fire was set, giving off a looming sense of grim events that were about to be set in motion.

The crackling of the fire made Corrin twinge as he remembered the burnt bodies he discovered on the new planet. He began losing his footing, but Evrii held him up.

She walked him over to the head of the table where his seat awaited him. Evrii sat next to him, waiting for Corrin to speak about what happened.

Corrin could tell everyone in the room was eager, concerned, and slightly nervous as to what happened to him out there.

He wasn't sure how he was going to tell them that he had put all their lives in danger. He wasn't sure how he was going to look into his wife's eyes and tell her that his actions might have doomed their children.

"Wi-Lao," Corrin said, finally speaking.

Wi-Lao stood from his seat. His black skin was covered in the tattoos that every warrior priest had. Tattoos that represented the culture of Wa-Rin. The dim fire reflected off his light blue eyes that he shared with his comrades. The long braid he sported on his shaved head rested on his shoulder, with the bottom of it brushing up against his orange drape.

"Yes, my lord" answered Wi-Lao.

"Enable all defenses around the atmosphere," Corrin said sternly, but with a hint of fear mixed in.

"Giro-Po, Fae-Zung, Sun-Tro," Corrin said.

They all stood immediately. Giro-Po's usual calm and spiritual-like demeanor was nowhere to be found. Fae-Zung's long blond hair covered most of her face, but her eyes were focused on Corrin. Sun-Tro's thin tan body stood firm as Corrin gave them their orders.

"Gather the rest of the warrior priests who are stationed across the planet. Bring them here at once."

Evrii's eyes were wide at hearing Corrin say all this. She looked across the table at Zhao-Lan, who returned her gaze with the same confused and concerned eyes. His fair skin glowed from the dim fire as his black-asmidnight hair swayed from a gust of wind. He watched with his light blue eyes as Evrii placed her hands on Corrin's arm and looked at him with pleading eyes.

"My love, please, tell us what this is all about. What happened?"

Corrin bowed his head before looking up at Evrii, then to Zhao-Lan and the other warrior priests.

"Arcadia, because of me, is now an enemy of The Black Palace!"

Low murmurs from the warrior priests filled the room. Evrii took her hands away from Corrin's arm. Her eyes were wider than ever now.

"I found the planets my Father wanted me to help add to the empire. But he had already begun his assault on those worlds."

Evrii, Zhao-Lan, and the other warrior priests listened in silence as Corrin painted with his words what he saw. Drisa-Yun, one of Corrin's fiercest warrior priests, had tears rolling down her face as Corrin told them about the little girl he couldn't save. Her curly purple hair couldn't mask the pain in her eyes. Evrii felt every bit of sadness in Corrin's voice as if she had seen everything as well. Corrin stood from his seat slowly, regaining his strength already.

"The All Father has stripped me of my titles and has labeled me a traitor to The Black Palace and the universe. I am an outlaw now, but that doesn't mean you all have to go down with me. When Wi-Lao has the defenses enabled and the other warrior priests arrive, you all can go home. My fight does not have to be yours!" Corrin said, his voice breaking.

Zhao-Lan stood up from his seat. "We are with you, Lord Corrin!"

Silence fell upon the room. The tension was so thick, not even the strongest blade wielded by the most skilled swordsman could cut it.

Fear began filling the room until the other warrior priests around the table stood up as well. The others in the room all nodded at Corrin as he looked around. They were with him.

He looked at Evrii as she stood up as well. Her teary eyes reassured him that she was with him till the end.

Later that night, as the light from Arcadia's moon battled the nighttime blanket over the capital city, Corrin flew up into the clouds to make sure the atmospheric defenses were in place to protect the planet from any retaliation The All Father would do.

The capital city of Arcadia, where the bulk of the population of the planet resided, sat in between two mountain ranges, giving the city a natural defense from land attacks but left them open to a sea invasion that could cause the citizens to be trapped by the mountains.

Corrin figured the capital would be the main target if his Father was to attack. All different types of scenarios played through Corrin's head. He had led his Father's army for years and knew how the military operated and all their tactics, but he knew his warrior priests wouldn't be enough to protect the entire planet from a full-scale invasion.

As he finished checking the defenses, he descended to the surface and landed on top of one of the mountain ranges looking over the city. Millions of souls beneath him were in their homes not knowing the amount of danger that lay just above them in the stars.

He overlooked the city in deep thought, before hearing someone approaching him from the rear. He thought he was alone and immediately turned to attack but stopped as he saw it was Evrii.

She giggled. "Luckily, I'm not your enemy, it would have ended badly for you," she said, putting her hands on Corrin's shoulders and joining him in overlooking the city.

They looked at the beautiful city they built together over the past twelve years. The first planet to host multiple inhabitants of different worlds in a safe, civilized, and prosperous society.

As they admired their achievement, fear of the future crept its way back into Corrin's peaceful moment, shattering the little time of peace he wouldn't have again for years to come.

"This city, this planet, our home, will suffer for my actions, Evrii," Corrin said, keeping his eyes fixated on the lights from the houses below.

Evrii placed her head on Corrin's shoulder and rubbed his back softly, trying her hardest to be a rock for the man she married.

"The people down there came here for a new life, a better way of living, and I promised them peace. But instead, I have broken their trust and have thrown them into the middle of a fight they did not choose."

Evrii could hear how broken Corrin was.

He looked at her. "Take the children and leave for Rashalon."

Evrii picked her head up from his shoulder and stepped back. "What?," she replied, shocked.

Corrin stepped forward and grabbed her. "Take the children and leave. They are not safe around me. You are not safe around me. Arcadia is not safe because of me. Don't you see, I *am* the Shepherd of Fire. Anywhere I go, everything I touch brings death. Halvodon. Syeron. Pugart. My mother!! I am my Father's son. I only represent *death*."

Evrii pulled her arms away from Corrin and slapped him in the face.

"How dare you?!" she said angrily. "You want me to abandon my home, my new people, *my husband*, because you are *afraid*?"

Corrin looked at her in silence.

"What about me, Corrin? You don't think I'm afraid? I am *terrified*! But my love and belief in you are greater than any trouble, any fear, and any threat The All Father makes!"

Evrii stepped up to Corrin and grabbed his face.

"You are so much more than what your Father has made you to believe! Whatever happens, we will face together!"

Tears fell down her cheeks as she stared into Corrin's eyes. Corrin tried holding back his tears but let them loose as he embraced Evrii, his love.

They held each other on top of the mountain as Arcadia fell into a beautiful sleep for the last time.

After their heart-to-heart on the mountain range, Corrin and Evrii went back to their home to sleep. But the realm of dreams did not let Corrin enter that night. His nerves were too wired for him to rest his head. He stayed up all night with Zhao-Lan and the other warrior priests, watching and waiting.

Back at The Black Palace, wards were gathering their belongings and rushing out of the Palace as The All Father was heard destroying everything upstairs.

"How dare he disrespect me!" The All Father yelled as things crashed around.

The Spear of Space radiated large amounts of energy as The All Father raged, almost giving off a sense of enjoyment to see, and or even feel, The All Father be out of control.

A Black Palace ward hid behind a fallen case of helmets worn by slain leaders and generals of different planets that had opposed The All Father.

"My liege, Father of All, Dyerian is here to see you," the ward said, trembling as The All Father punched through a metal pillar of rebel weapons melted down into a war trophy.

The All Father whipped his head around to the ward, piercing him with his glowing white glare.

The ward gulped and ran out as Dyerian walked into the room. Grater followed behind him and was in shock to see how in shambles the almighty All Father's chambers had become.

Both of them knelt before The All Father as he took a seat on a chair missing an armrest.

"As of tonight, and so forth, Corrin is an enemy of The Black Palace," The All Father said.

To him, it felt out of place to call his own son an enemy.

Grater also lifted his bowed head at the sound of it. Dyerian smiled to himself.

"Any Arcadian seen, including my son's band of monks," The All Father said, attempting to insult the warrior priests and take away their prestige as talented killers, "are hereby ordered to be executed on the spot!"

Grater gulped and spoke out, his voice shaking slightly.

"And what of Lord Corrin, All Father?" Grater asked.

The All Father sat silent for a moment before Dyerian spoke.

"He said *all* Arcadians!"

Dyerian stood up and placed his fist on his chest.

"Allow me to lead your forces into Arcadia to kill Corrin and bring you his head, my liege!"

Grater looked up at him wide-eyed. He feared The All Father would agree to this. Instead, The All Father stood up and shut down Dyerian's request.

"I allowed my son to speak to me as my superior with requests and he is now a traitor. I will not let a Fargulkian not of my blood, especially a commander in my military, ask demands of me!" The All Father said sternly, glaring at Dyerian.

"My liege, I-I meant no—" Dyerian started, but was cut off.

"*Silence*. Corrin is not to be harmed until I say so," The All Father said, sitting back down.

Dyerian knelt again, embarrassed but visibly angry. Angry not at The All Father, but at Corrin, for once again being ahead.

"You two will join General Nafo-Veguz on the expedition to claim the new worlds. My new worlds!"

Grater kept his eyes low but could almost feel Dyerian's pulsating veins at the sound of the two of them being sent to invade worlds instead of killing Corrin. They both stood and left The All Father's chambers to prepare.

As daylight crept onto Arcadia, the warrior priests and Corrin continued their overnight watch of the planet.

Corrin could tell some of the warrior priests were on edge. Although skilled in the art of combat and masters of channeling spear energy, most of them had never seen battle or been in a serious altercation other than training exercises.

The mix of fear of The All Father with the lack of sleep danced on the faces of the men and women Corrin considered his most trustworthy allies.

Evrii watched from the balcony as the rest of the warrior priests arrived from the east, bringing along with them Lynn and Kale.

Corrin looked up at the balcony to see Evrii watching Lynn and Kale running on the shore to greet their mother. Seeing his family together brought him peace but that sense of peace was shattered.

Horns blared from the atmosphere, able to be heard around the entire planet of Arcadia. Evrii held Kale and Lynn as she stared at Corrin in absolute fear.

In the city, citizens of Arcadia scrambled from the streets and markets as they rushed to their homes. Corrin and the warrior priests ran to the edge of a cliff as a few other warrior priests descended from the clouds.

"Lord Corrin," one of them yelled from the sky. *"Black Palace fleet is approaching Arcadia! It's an invasion!"*

Corrin felt a cold gust of wind hit the back of his neck. He was frozen still in shock before breaking out of the trance.

"Ready all defenses," Corrin yelled to the warrior priests behind him. "Remember, Arcadia cannot be destroyed. This invasion is targeted toward the people. They are our main priority. We must keep the fight off-world!"

A squadron of warrior priests, led by Sun-Tro, charged up their energy and blasted into the sky, heading toward the scattered turret defense systems in the atmosphere.

Zhao-Lan and a few other warrior priests jumped off the cliff and zoomed toward the city to make sure the citizens of Arcadia were safe. Corrin and the rest prepared to launch into space.

As the warrior priests and Corrin charged up, Corrin looked back at his home and saw Evrii rushing Kale and Lynn inside.

"For Arcadia!" Corrin yelled, as he and the rest of the warrior priests ran toward the cliff and blasted into the sky.

As they all broke through the clouds and through the atmosphere, The All Father's invasion fleet approached closer. Corrin's heart raced as the ships neared the planet.

He knew Arcadia was created to withstand any outside destruction, even from the Spear of Space, but he knew the people below would perish if the battle landed on its surface.

"This is where we hold them!" Corrin yelled back to the warrior priests behind him.

As the ships got closer and closer, the warrior priests arming the defense turrets gripped the trigger handles.

Silence fell upon the universe for a moment. But something was off.

Corrin knew the military tactics of an invasion and how the army reacted to enemy combatants in its path.

"Something's not right," Corrin said.

He knew that the ships wouldn't get this close without firing already. The invasion fleet reached the planet, but instead of firing on Corrin and the warrior priests, and instead of tactically firing on Arcadia's defense systems, the fleet kept moving forward. The fleet passed over Arcadia, blocking out the morning sun, and casting an ominous shadow over the planet.

From the streets, Zhao-Lan and the other warrior priests looked up in confusion. Evrii peered out from her window as the fleet continued its path forward.

As the fleet passed over Arcadia, Corrin flew back down to the surface. As he landed, Zhao-Lan and Evrii ran up to meet him.

"What's happening?" Evrii asked.

"Is this some sort of ploy? Are we being deceived?" Zhao-Lan asked as the rest of the warrior priests descended from the clouds and came from the streets.

Corrin pondered for a moment under the shadow of the fleet.

"No," he said. "The military doesn't operate that way. They wouldn't amass a fleet this large for a distraction."

Corrin turned and looked into the sky.

"Then, where are they going?" asked Fae-Zung.

Corrin's eyes widened.

"The new worlds!" he said.

Corrin quickly turned to Evrii and the warrior priests. He looked into all their eyes.

"Are you with me?!" he asked them.

Zhao-Lan stepped forward and charged up his energy. All the other warrior priests did the same. Corrin turned and ran toward the cliff. All the warrior priests from Arcadia followed him. As they reached the end of the cliff, they all blasted into the sky, through the clouds, and into space, zooming toward the new worlds.

Corrin and the warrior priests passed the invasion fleet, their collective force rocking the ships.

Dyerian and Grater were on board the main ship with General Nafo-Veguz. General Nafo-Veguz was born and raised on Eqoulis. Eqoulis was a massive desert planet. The inhabitants would usually leave for a better or different world due to Eqoulis only having two areas of civilization with limited resources.

General Nafo-Veguz stood tall, almost passing for a Fargulkian. His dark green hair was long and thick. His orange eyes spoke of reverence and prestige as his wrinkled maroon skin was covered in majestic Black Palace armor. His armor was decorated with medals and trophies of war, which he earned throughout his service during the Itarian era.

"You should have struck them when we had the advantage, General!" Dyerian said, as the light from Corrin's and the warrior priest's energies zoomed past them.

General Nafo-Veguz clenched his jaw.

"When you're a decorated warrior like me, Fargulkian, then you can give the orders," General Nafo-Veguz said, as he turned and left the main ship's cockpit.

Dyerian snarled his nostrils as Nafo-Veguz walked away.

Grater peered out the ship's window as the light from Corrin's and the warrior priest's energies faded in the distance.

"If you want to join that traitor and embarrassment, go ahead!" Dyerian said, stepping up to the glass. He pulled out a blade. "But go quickly, before I slit your throat right here!"

Grater turned to face Dyerian, trying to show he wasn't intimidated by the Fargulkian's words or size.

But he was.

Dyerian stared down at him. Grater tried to hold out but looked away.

"Good!" Dyerian said, before leaving the cockpit.

Grater looked back out the window into deep space, conflicted about his loyalty to The All Father and to Corrin, his best friend.

The warrior priests and Corrin zoomed past the known worlds.

Inhabitants on Catovaz looked up into their sky as the collective energies of Corrin and the warrior priests flew past the planet.

They zoomed past Myero, Scav, Di, and Jargun-Ba like a giant comet, trying to get to the new worlds before the fleet.

As they passed the known worlds, the invasion fleet followed quickly, picking up speed and casting a looming, but familiar shadow over the conquered planets in The All Father's planetary kingdom.

As they reached the first new world, the planet where he found the remains of the inhabitants and the little girl, Corrin stopped in mid-space.

"We hold the line here. Farther out are the new worlds that do not need to be victim to my Father's wrath," Corrin said as the warrior priests formed a barrier. They floated in the blackness of the universe, the new worlds behind them.

At The Black Palace, The All Father could feel the tension brewing in space. He went to grab the Spear of Space to intervene but stopped himself. Something inside him was holding him back from unleashing his full power to end what he considered his son's disobedience.

Back where the clash between Corrin, the warrior priests, and the invasion fleet was imminent, General Nafo-Veguz ordered the ships to prepare to fire.

As the weapons on the ship began turning toward Corrin and the warrior priests, Corrin spoke quickly.

"The men on board those ships are pawns to my Father's game. Disable the ships. Take no lives if you can."

The blasters on the ship were officially pointed at Corrin and the warrior priests.

"Hold this line!" Corrin yelled.

The warrior priests began charging up their energy.

On board the main ship, Dyerian watched eagerly as Grater feared for what was about to happen.

As the warrior priests formed shields of energy, General Nafo-Veguz lifted his hand.

"Fire!"

Blasters from the fleet exploded toward Corrin and the warrior priests. The energy shield the warrior priests had formed was holding.

Dyerian snarled from inside the ship as the blasters did nothing to Corrin's defense.

"Move the ships closer, General! *Penetrate their shield!*" Dyerian yelled.

General Nafo-Veguz knew that if the fleet was any closer, it would penetrate the shield, possibly killing

Corrin and going against The All Father's order to not harm him. He also knew that getting the ships any closer would give Corrin and the warrior priests an easier advantage to strike the fleet's weapons.

Corrin knew this as well and waited to see what the general of the fleet would do as the blasters had no effect on the energy shield. Warrior priests yelled as blasts from the fleet bounced off the shield wall.

General Nafo-Veguz contemplated what do before giving the order to move forward.

As the ships moved forward, the blasters began penetrating the shield wall, hitting and killing warrior priests. Their lifeless bodies were launched back and sucked into the orbit and down to the surface of the new world below them.

Corrin watched in anguish as his warriors fell and released a powerful yell, *"Now!"*

The warrior priests all yelled together as they broke the shield wall and zoomed toward the ships.

Corrin led the advancement, evading blast after blast. Zhao-Lan formed an energy ball around him as he zoomed through a blast from one the fleet's weapons.

Warrior priests were evading blast after blast as well as they zoomed toward the fleet, some getting hit and launching backward. Some exploded in mid-space, their body parts floating off.

As Corrin reached the first ship, he pulled out his sword and sliced through it, creating a deep gash along the entire side of it.

As the ship malfunctioned, Black Palace soldiers from inside jumped out and battled warrior priests.

Wi-Lao and Drisa-Yun formed energy blades and sliced through another ship, splitting it in two.

General Nafo-Veguz gave the order for the rest of The Black Palace infantry to attack. Soldiers burst out of the ships and into open space. Unlike the warrior priests, the Black Palace Soldiers needed space suits in order to engage in battle with the warrior priests. The suits made The Black Palace soldiers slower but more resilient to energy blasts from the warrior priests.

Trained in the art of combat since birth, and masters of the cosmic arts, the warrior priests easily dominated the Black Palace soldiers. However the soldier's numbers gave them a slight edge.

Corrin continued slicing through the rest of the ships, trying to disable as many as he could. Black Palace soldiers swarmed him as he cut through Gorkonian metal, but he launched them back, trying his hardest not to kill any of them.

Warrior priests were fighting Black Palace soldiers hand-to-hand, evading their blades and side blasters, and either knocking them out or blasting them back toward the ships that hadn't been destroyed yet.

General Nafo-Veguz watched in discomfort as Corrin and the warrior priests ripped through the ships. Grater watched in awe, trying not to smile. Dyerian was putting on his armor, his eyes fixated on Corrin through the glass.

As he was about to exit the ship, General Nafo-Veguz yelled over the main ship's intercom, *"Retreat!"*

Dyerian turned in anger and disgust and stormed up to the intercom, slamming it off.

"*Retreat?* We outnumber them!"

General Nafo-Veguz looked back out into space, seeing his fleet being destroyed and his men definitely outnumbering the warrior priests but doing no significant damage.

"We were ordered to invade, not engage in battle with Lord Corrin. If we somehow survive, you can explain to The All Father why one of his fleets was destroyed and *why* you disobeyed a general!" General Nafo-Veguz said, glaring at Dyerian.

Dyerian looked into his eyes angrily, until realizing he feared The All Father more than he desired to finally fight Corrin. Grater looked at them both in shock, waiting to see what would happen. General Nafo-Veguz kept his eyes on Dyerian, his hand still on the intercom.

Dyerian let out a grunt and stormed off to his chambers.

General Nafo-Veguz again gave the order to retreat. Black Palace soldiers glided back to the ships as the fleet began to turn back toward The Black Palace.

The warrior priests yelled with strength at the sight of the fleet leaving. Wi-Lao grabbed Drisa-Yun and kissed her as Zhao-Lan ordered other warrior priests to check on the wounded.

Corrin stood in the midst of the celebrating warrior priests, examining the results of the battle. Destroyed Black Palace ships continued to malfunction as bodies of dead warrior priests were recovered. Corrin felt lucky to still be breathing but feared that this was just the beginning of something he knew would cost him everything.

CHAPTER 9

LINES ARE DRAWN

On Arcadia, Evrii waited eagerly for word about the battle. She paced back and forth in a nervous manner wondering if Corrin had won or not. Kale and Lynn watched from afar as their mother twirled her thumbs.

"Mother," Lynn said.

Evrii turned to Lynn and noticed both children were feeding off her anxiety. She rushed over and tried to reassure them that everything was going to be okay. As she held her children, Evrii couldn't help but feel an overbearing sense of dread consume her.

The sun of Arcadia was getting ready to set and citizens of the planet were all on edge, all concerned and scared about Corrin having left with the warrior priests.

Evrii continued holding her children, trying to calm their fears just as much as she was trying to calm hers.

Yelling from the streets shocked her. She ran to the balcony to look down at the city where the yelling was coming from. The Arcadians were all pointing up to the sky as a collective beam of energy broke through the planet's atmosphere.

Kale and Lynn ran up to the balcony to watch as well.

Evrii's purple eyes glimmered from the light of the energy as she let out a sigh of relief.

"Your father is home," she said, staring up into the sky as the beam of energy landed on the cliff near the edge of the city, revealing Corrin and the warrior priests.

The battered warrior priests and Corrin quickly took the wounded to Arcadia's healers. Zhao-Lan rushed over to the planet's guards to make sure everything was prepared just in case The All Father decided to attack.

Many of the warrior priests had taken heavy hits from The Black Palace forces, leaving Corrin's only defense against The All Father extremely weakened.

Evrii rushed over to Corrin, who was covered in minor battle wounds. He was checking up on the injured, being the leader he was meant to be.

"My love," Evrii said, looking Corrin up and down in disbelief.

Corrin was happy to see her. He embraced her, holding her tight as if he hadn't seen her in ages.

"We took heavy losses," Corrin solemnly said, looking around at the wounded warrior priests and wondering if their blood was worth this skirmish against The All Father.

Evrii could tell Corrin was in distress but held strong for him.

"They are with you, Corrin," Evrii said, reassuring him. "I am with you!"

Corrin took solace in hearing her say that.

Later that night, Corrin walked through the infirmary, checking up on the wounded warriors. He knew this would be the first of many battles. The first of many casualties. He didn't want to risk an all-out war with The All Father.

But back at The Black Palace, sentiments of war were already brewing.

"Nafo-Veguz led a disastrous campaign to the new worlds, endangering his men, and showing vulnerability amongst our ranks," touted a man seated at a table with twelve other men.

"General Kartov is right," chimed in another man.

"General Nafo-Veguz, how could you let this happen?!"

The other men all looked at General Nafo-Veguz, who was sitting at the far end of the table. He had shame written all over his face but answered with dignity and pride.

These generals had been a part of the Itarian empire during The Long Sleep. When The All Father awoke and made his proclamation across the universe of his return, he slaughtered the current Itarian leader and his kin, promising the universe an era of peace and freedom. He recruited military strategists, commanders, generals, and advisors who had served under the Itarian emperors and had them form his military. These men from all worlds witnessed the might of The All Father and the Spear, and did not hesitate, either out of fear or lust for power, to fall in line.

"I had direct orders from The All Father to not kill Lord Corrin. I did my duty, just as any of you would have," he said, keeping his composure.

"Corrin," Dyerian said, sitting away from the table with Grater.

"He is just Corrin now, General! No respective titles. Maybe if you remembered that, you wouldn't have lost!"

Murmurs across the table rang throughout the room.

General Nafo-Veguz shot up from his chair, about to react to Dyerian's disrespect of his rank until The All Father walked in with Moira by his side.

All the men stopped their chattering as The All Father made his way to the head of the table. General Nafo-Veguz sank back into his seat, glaring at Dyerian.

Dyerian smirked back at him.

As The All Father sat down, silence fell around the room. None of the generals wanted to make eye contact with him. General Nafo-Veguz sat directly across from The All Father, trying his hardest not to show fear on his face.

After a dragged-out moment of silence, The All Father spoke.

"So," he said, looking around the table. "My son has taken up arms against me."

No one in the room spoke.

Grater looked around. He never thought he'd be in a room where The All Father and his most trusted advisors and generals were talking about Corrin, his best friend, as an enemy.

He looked at Moira, who was staring back at him.

The All Father clenched his jaw.

"Do any of you have a solution to this?" he asked. His irritation could be felt in his words.

General Kartov rose from his seat. His Black Palace armor was decorated with medals and trophies of war. He was aged and had heavy battle scars on his face. He cleared his throat.

"If I may speak, my liege. I believe General Nafo-Veguz's embarrassing defeat allows us to spin this failure to our advantage."

The All Father was confused. "Continue," he said, cutting his eyes to General Nafo-Veguz.

"The bulk of Lord, I mean, Corrin's forces are said to have been wounded. His army of magicians…" General Kartov let out a laugh.

Some of the other men around the table laughed as well. The All Father didn't.

"…have taken serious damage. Now's the time to continue onward to the new worlds, solidify your presence in the worlds within the empire, and show no mercy to any who dares rally against you."

General Kartov sat back down in his seat. Heads nodding in agreement moved around the table.

Another man stood up. "General Kartov is right. Corrin is outnumbered, outgunned, and doesn't have the resources to ignite another attack. If we continue on as planned, we'll have the new worlds under your control within days."

The man sat back down.

The All Father didn't show any notion of agreement or disagreement.

Another man stood up. "General Kartov and General Urix are correct."

More generals stood up in agreement.

They all agreed that maintaining control of the empire and proceeding as planned was the best course of action.

Dyerian didn't.

"You all are wrong," Dyerian said, standing up from his seat.

Grater sighed.

All the generals looked at him and scoffed.

General Nafo-Veguz glared at him.

"Now is the perfect time to attack Arcadia and destroy Corrin and the rest of his men," Dyerian exclaimed.

"And risk all the other worlds rallying behind him as a martyr? Risk a planetary rebellion? Are you mad?" General Kartov said, ridiculing Dyerian's plan.

"If we don't extinguish him now, we risk the worlds rallying behind him while he's alive! You think he's more dangerous dead. But I'm telling you, he's just as dangerous if left alive."

General Kartov glared at Dyerian, swallowing hard.

The All Father rose from his seat. All the generals straightened out.

He looked into all their eyes. He stared at Dyerian, who didn't cut his eyes away. He looked at General Nafo-Veguz.

"You have been quiet, General," The All Father said.

General Nafo-Veguz straightened out even more before he spoke. "I believe General Kartov and all of your other advisors are correct in their assessment. Corrin does not pose a threat anymore and we should secure the planets and move forward on acquiring the new worlds!"

Dyerian rolled his eyes.

Grater let out a sigh of relief.

"It's decided, then. We continue as planned. Double our forces on every planet. Show our strength. Bring the new worlds to my command. The Black Palace is the only force in this universe!"

The All Father walked out of the room. The men around the table began dispersing and chatting.

General Kartov walked up to Dyerian.

"If you ever speak out against me in front of The All Father again, I'll have you skinned and your dying body thrown to the savages on Jargun-Ba."

General Kartov stormed off. Dyerian was fuming through his clenched jaw. Moira walked up to him.

"Bold," she said. "If you want Corrin dead, you'll have to get in line," she said flirtatiously, smiling with her eyes at Dyerian.

"Hello, Grater," she continued, looking down at Grater who was sitting there out of place.

Grater didn't make eye contact with her but responded anyway.

"Hello, Moira," he said disgusted.

He couldn't bring himself to look into the eyes of someone he had once considered a close friend. Someone who turned their back on Corrin out of a grudge.

"Don't look so sad, Grater. Eventually Corrin will be dead and maybe The All Father will give you that Rasho whore he calls a wife," Moira said, walking away pleased with herself.

During the Twelve Good Years, Moira had never gotten over how Corrin had picked Evrii over her. She has spent her time doing anything she can to get back at him for breaking her heart.

On Arcadia, a few days had gone by since the battle for the new worlds. The warrior priests, Corrin, and the citizens of Arcadia had all been on edge, preparing and waiting to see if The All Father was going to attack or not.

Whispers of unidentified ships heading Arcadia's way reached Corrin, making him wonder if his Father was going to try to invade Arcadia in a stealth attack, bypassing the planet's defense systems.

Zhao-Lan approached Corrin, who was already showing stress and worry in his eyes.

"We have multiple ships approaching Arcadia. They're not Black Palace. Would The All Father try to trick us?"

"No," Corrin responded. "Let them pass."

Zhao-Lan signaled for the atmospheric guards to allow the ships to enter Arcadia's orbit.

Corrin and Zhao-Lan waited intensely as the guards identified those who came to Arcadia unannounced. A few moments passed before one of the guards radioed back down to Corrin and Zhao-Lan.

"They're emissaries from Fargulk, Kaasiar, Aoweii, Scav, Telamor, and Yres," the guard said. The shock, surprise, and excitement were clear in his voice.

Zhao-Lan and Corrin both looked at each other, confused but eager to see what this was about.

All the emissaries gathered in the mess hall with Corrin, Evrii, and Zhao-Lan.

The emissaries were chatting and arguing. They came from planets that had bad histories with one another. Deep resentment and unresolved issues from the Itarian era still haunted them.

But nonetheless, they had all managed to come together to see Corrin.

As the arguing and yelling continued, Corrin looked at Evrii, who gave him a concerned look. He looked back at the crowd.

One of the emissaries finally spoke up from the noise, addressing Corrin. "Lord Corrin."

The yelling and arguing stopped.

A man wearing purple armor and a yellow cloak stepped forward. He was holding his helmet, showing his dark brown skin and bald head.

"I am General Dalire of Kaasiar. My home planet is ready to pledge its allegiance and full military to you!"

Kaasiar was a large green planet. A forest world of valleys, trees, and plains that stretched for miles.

General Dalire looked at Corrin fiercely with his light velvet eyes. He wore his valor on his sleeve and had the hope of a free Kaasiar, and a free universe, written on his face.

"The five kingdoms of Yres are ready to stand with you, Lord Corrin! Your mother's home world has lived long enough in the shadow of the The All Father," a woman declared.

She stood tall. Her pale translucent skin paid homage to the sea people of Yres.

"I am General Gaffen. The five kings of Yres have united their navies and have instructed me to inform you that the navy is yours!"

Corrin sat silently, taking this all in. The last time he visited Yres was when he was a boy to see where his mother was born and raised. The blue planet covered by water was now here to aid him against his own Father.

Zhao-Lan and Evrii looked at each other, with Evrii now amazed to hear all this.

"I am Amoz Moza, Lord Corrin. I have spoken with emissary Rolyn of Fargulk and emissary Sergex of Scav, and I speak on behalf of Taelvum. We are all ready to lend you our fiercest warriors."

The emissary from Aoweii sat patiently, waiting to hear what Corrin had to say.

"I am flattered and beyond grateful for all of you traveling here. But I cannot ask you to give your sons and daughters to this fight. This is my fight and my fight alone. I cannot in good conscience involve innocent lives."

The generals and emissaries were taken aback.

Evrii looked at Zhao-Lan. Zhao-Lan took Corrin aside. Evrii followed.

"We need all the forces we can get, my lord," Zhao-Lan said.

"Zhao-Lan is right, my love. We cannot win this alone."

Corrin looked at Evrii confused.

"Win what? I do not want to go to war with my Father."

He turned away from Zhao-Lan and Evrii, addressing the generals and emissaries again.

"Return to your homes. Bunker down. I am sorry, but this is not your fight or a fight I asked for."

As Corrin turned away, the emissary from Aoweii stood up.

"Forgive me, Lord Corrin, if I may."

Corrin turned back around.

"You say this is not our fight, but it is," the emissary from Aoweii stated.

The other generals and emissaries looked at him, listening.

"It's been our fight since the beginning. Ever since The All Father awoke from his sleep and lost your mother, he began a campaign across our universe to command every planet under an iron fist. Any movement to end his reign has always ended quickly with any opposition being violently snuffed out. Even by your hand."

That last part made Corrin uncomfortable.

The emissary from Aoweii continued, "But now, someone has fought The All Father and won. With all our differences and past tribulations, your transgressions aligned us and gave us the hope and singular purpose we've been looking for. Liberation. You're known as the Shepherd of Fire across the galaxies. Become the Shepherd of Freedom."

Corrin gulped. He didn't want to involve others in his fight against his Father. He didn't even want to fight in the first place. But deep down he knew that something had been sparked and would eventually turn into a flame of uncertainty. He knew that if he was going to fight his Father, he couldn't win alone. He needed the help of the other planets.

"If we do this, it needs to be strategic and the loss of life minimal."

Evrii perked up. Zhao-Lan let out a small smile.

The emissary from Aoweii bowed his head. The other generals and emissaries cheered.

Corrin approached the emissary from Aoweii and shook his hand. "I didn't catch your name."

"I am Emoran of Aoweii."

Corrin, Evrii, and Zhao-Lan were dumbfounded.

Aoweii was one of the oldest planets in the universe. It was an elf-like planet with elite warriors who were able to withstand the Itarian empire in the eighth cycle.

"Aoweii never gets involved in outer world problems," Corrin said, confused.

"It's time for the universe to stand together once again against a common enemy," Emoran said.

"Lord Corrin," General Dalire said, interrupting. "I will travel with Amoz, Rolyn, and Sergex to Taelvum, Fargulk, and Scav to get their warriors. We will rendezvous with the army of Kaasiar and return soon."

Corrin nodded, giving them leave.

"The United Navy of Yres will be on-world waiting for your command. If battle comes, we will be prepared," General Gaffen said before leaving to her ship.

"Will Aoweii's army be rendezvousing here as well?" Evrii asked Emoran.

"No," he said. "The army will be staying on-world to protect the planet from other elements we are dealing with. Aoweii will, however, be lending you our best strategic advisors and a small specialized force led by our chief's daughter, Morgana."

Zhao-Lan chimed in, "A small specialized force led by the chief's daughter? Is that enough? You just said this is all our fight, but you won't be aiding us with an army?"

"Zhao-Lan." Corrin turned and gave him a stern look.

"A small specialized force that can take out an entire army and destabilize a planet overnight," Emoran said. "Morgana will be here soon."

Emoran placed his hands on Corrin's shoulders.

"Stay strong, Lord Corrin, dark days are ahead of us," Emoran said, leaving to his ship.

Corrin turned to face Evrii and Zhao-Lan, the fear of uncertainty on his face. "Let's prepare!"

As the emissaries left Arcadia, Zaman entered The Black Palace for the first time since its creation.

Wards, residents, and guards looked at him in shock and awe as he stormed his way to The All Father's quarters. No one had ever seen Zaman before, but his presence gave off a massive sense of importance. His glowing white eyes resembled those of The All Father, and his light blue skin glowed under The Black Palace moon. His long cloak dragged across the metallic floors. He had anger in his eyes.

"Nox," Zaman yelled, as he pushed through the doors.

Generals, advisors, and quarter wards all turned in shock. No one had ever addressed The All Father by his first name.

Zaman pushed through the crowded room and reached The All Father, who was seated on a makeshift throne of conquered kings' helmets from the Itarian era.

"What is the meaning of this, Nox?" Zaman demanded.

The room kept chatting, but eyes were darting back and forth to the two Spear holders.

The All Father stood, towering over Zaman. He pushed away an outer barrier girl from Kkooddrraa and embraced Zaman with laughter.

He was in a cheerful mood.

"Zaman, my oldest friend, what is all this ruckus? Come, we are celebrating the acquisition of the new worlds."

Zaman was not in a celebratory mood. He had heard about the battle between The All Father and Corrin and was worried about the fate of the universe.

"Now is not the time for games, Nox," Zaman said, pushing him away.

The room fell completely quiet. Everyone stared at Zaman and The All Father. No one would ever dare put their hands on the creator, let alone think they would do it and survive.

The All Father could feel all eyes on him as the room anticipated his next move. The Spear of Space began radiating, giving off the same energy the Spear of Time gave to Zaman.

"Everyone out, now!" The All Father demanded, keeping his eyes on Zaman, who was staring right back into his.

As the room cleared, Zaman lifted his hand, calling for the Spear of Time. It came zooming to him in a blink of an eye.

"You and Corrin must end your differences immediately," Zaman pleaded.

The All Father scoffed, turning away to return to his seat.

"Nox, you must understand. The Spears are trying to speak to us. The energy they've been putting out is because of a rise in tension between you and your son. That is what the Spear of Time was trying to tell me. Trying to warn us. It's the only explanation."

The All Father knew deep down in his heart that Zaman was right. But he couldn't fight his ego. To him, Corrin had embarrassed him enough. He needed to put his son back in place.

"You speak as if I am at fault for Corrin's betrayal. I am not. I am doing that for which I was created. Lead and conquer is what the Spear has bestowed me to do."

The All Father was getting angry.

"Your conquering and leadership are moving the universe toward a path of uncertainty. This leads only to chaos," Zaman said, trying to make The All Father understand.

The All Father sat quiet for a little while. Zaman began to believe that what he was saying was starting to resonate with The All Father.

"I see," The All Father said. Then he laughed, and narrowed his eyes at Zaman. "Before now, you never involved yourself with my affairs. But now that my son is challenging me, you come here on his behalf."

Zaman couldn't believe what he was hearing.

"Nox, have you gone mad? This isn't about you or Corrin, or me. It's about yielding power beyond our imagination in our hands and playing with it uncontrollably. You must end this now!"

The All Father leaped from his seat and called for the Spear of Space in midair. He floated above Zaman, his demeanor now that of a God.

"You dare command me, Zaman? You forget your place, Time Keeper!"

Zaman floated up to The All Father, yielding the Spear of Time in his hand. His eyes began radiating just as powerful as The All Father.

"I am not one of your subjects you can force fear into, Nox. I was created just like you and yield a Spear just as powerful as yours."

The two stared at each other. Their white eyes matched each other's energy. The aura in the room thickened. The Spears were radiating out of control, almost as if they were being pulled to each other.

"You know what happens if the Spears touch, Nox. Everything you've built gone. This universe eradicated in the blink of an eye. We don't even know if either us will survive if the Spears were to clash once again."

The All Father glared at Zaman. He knew if they fought it would risk the total destruction of everything he had created. After another moment of wondering what to do, The All Father descended to the ground. Zaman followed.

The All Father turned back to his throne.

"Go back to your sanctuary, Time Keeper. Stay out of my way!"

Zaman let out a sigh and turned away to leave. As he reached the door, he turned back to Nox. "This is my final warning."

Sick of all the defiance, The All Father took offense to Zaman saying that and leaped at him. Zaman spun, evading The All Father's grasp. He threw the Spear of Time across the room, lodging it into the ground.

As The All Father lunged at Zaman again, he ducked and sprang up, grabbing The All Father by the head and putting him into a state of trance.

The All Father's glowing white eyes exploded with an influx of spear energy. Visions of destruction, terror, pain, and anguish flooded The All Father's consciousness.

Zaman released him, stepping back as The All Father collapsed to the floor. He called for the Spear of Time, which came racing back into his hand.

"You now see where your ego will take this universe. Choose wisely, Nox. I will not entertain this anymore!"

Zaman left The Black Palace, leaving The All Father on his hands and knees.

He glared at the ground, visualizing the images Zaman showed him. He lifted his head, looking at the Spear of Space and feeling its energy pull him in deeper.

CHAPTER 10

WAR IN THE UNIVERSE

With the news of Corrin's win spreading quickly across the universe, the planets under The All Father's control began rebelling. Black Palace soldiers were being targeted while magistrates and provincial governors were being dragged out of their stolen homes and murdered in the streets. The people felt the inspiration of Corrin going against The All Father and used that burning hope to fight back.

Catovaz was the first planet to massacre all of its Black Palace diplomats and declare full independence. The All Father began doubling the soldier count, scrambling to take back control of his kingdom.

Anti-Father posters were seen popping up in every city and province, instigating more attacks on Black Palace soldiers and All Father loyalists.

Back on Arcadia, more planets sent emissaries to join Corrin's cause.

"Catovaz has declared full independence from The All Father," Drisa-Yun said to Corrin, who was looking over schematics and battle plans with Zhao-Lan.

Corrin looked up, shocked and concerned, but also impressed.

"Send word to whoever is in charge there now. Let them know Arcadia stands with them and could use any support Catovaz can lend," Corrin said to Drisa-Yun.

"He's called Franzo Osaniz. He's calling himself emperor now," Drisa-Yun said.

Corrin and Zhao-Lan looked at each other, letting out a laugh.

"Of course he is," Corrin said, writing something down, then handing it to Drisa-Yun.

"Let the emperor know we could use Catovaz's courage and ice warriors."

Drisa-Yun took the note, nodded, and took off.

"Emperor, huh? Is everyone going to declare supremacy over their lands now?" Zhao-Lan asked, mocking the new ruler of Catovaz.

Corrin went back to look over the battle plans. "It's their land, Zhao-Lan. They must be free to choose what's best for them," Corrin said, pointing at a planet on the map.

"Here. This is where our forces should go first. Pugart!"

Zhao-Lan disregarded what Corrin said and continued, "It should be you to rule after this is all over. It has always been you."

Corrin looked away. He wished Zhao-Lan hadn't said that.

"You were born to lead, Corrin. This is your destiny!"

Corrin looked up. Flustered. "I don't want to rule trillions of souls, Zhao-Lan. This is not about exchanging one dominant ruler for another. This is about liberation. Freedom. Allowing the worlds to dictate their own paths."

Zhao-Lan persisted, "You won't be like your Father. You would be different. You would bring harmony to this universe."

Corrin had enough. "No more talk of this, Zhao-Lan. It is not what I want. Do not mention your opinions to anyone else. Please!"

Zhao-Lan clenched his jaw but agreed.

As they both went back to looking over the schematics, Evrii walked in.

"Lynn and Kale have been asking for you," she said, looking at Corrin with concerned eyes.

"I will see them soon," he said, looking up at Evrii, then back down to the schematics, and then back up to Evrii.

"Why aren't you in your armor?"

She looked at Zhao-Lan, who knew it was time to leave them in privacy for a moment.

As Zhao-Lan left, Evrii walked up to Corrin and placed her hands on his back. Corrin was confused, he thought Evrii was going to join him on the battlefield.

He turned to her. "You're not coming?" he asked, pushing her hair to the side.

Evrii caressed Corrin's arms.

"I am going to stay with the children. They need to be protected."

"I'll have our best warrior priests stay with them. They will be protected at all costs," Corrin pleaded.

"No one will protect them like their mother. I'm staying here. They need me. And Arcadia needs someone here to give them peace of mind."

Corrin wished to fight this war with Evrii by his side. Her strength on the battlefield rivaled any man's, but her inner strength that Corrin depended on was worth so much more.

As the two held each other, an applause rang through the chambers.

"Bravo. Almost brought tears to my eyes," a voice said.

Corrin and Evrii looked up to the ceiling. A woman was perched on one of the pillars. She jumped down and landed in front of them. Evrii grabbed a letter opener and put it to the woman's neck.

"Tell us who you are before you can't speak anymore," Evrii said, glaring into the woman's eyes.

The woman put her hands up, giggling. She had dark red hair flowing to her side. The other side of her head was shaved with a single long braid. Corrin could tell from her bright green eyes she was enjoying this.

"Relax, my lady, you'd be dead before my body hit the floor," the woman said, motioning with her eyes around the room.

Corrin and Evrii looked around and saw more figures appear out of the shadows in the ceiling, all pointing what looked like glowing bows and arrows at them.

Corrin didn't know what was going on and was about to attack before the woman grabbed the letter opener from Evrii and pointed it at her.

Corrin lunged at the woman. He swung at her and tried to grab her, but she evaded him with ease.

The other figures from the pillars jumped down and surrounded Evrii, who was now greatly outnumbered.

Corrin and the woman kept fighting. It looked more like a dance because Corrin couldn't land a single hit on her.

The other figures circled Evrii, their glowing bows and arrows illuminated their white-gold armor and blue face coverings. Corrin noticed them closing in on Evrii and let out a yell.

"Enough!" he said, releasing a blast of energy from his hands, sending the woman flying back.

He flew to the figures surrounding Evrii and blasted them away. His white eye was glowing.

Evrii ran to sound the alarm.

Corrin hovered above the woman and other figures. His hands were pulsating with energy.

"You will tell me now who you are or you will all die here today!"

The woman stood up from the ground.

The other figures were still pointing their glowing bows and arrows at Corrin.

"Impressive. You really are something magnificent. Emoran was right," the woman said.

Corrin's white eye stopped glowing and the energy from his hands withered away. He lowered himself to the ground.

"Emoran? Are you Morgana?" Corrin asked.

"Yes," Morgana responded, stepping forward and extending her hand to Corrin. "We are here to fight."

Corrin stood there for a moment, confused. He extended his hand and shook Morgana's.

Evrii came running in with the warrior priests. Zhao-Lan came in from the other door with more.

"What is this?" Evrii asked, confused.

The warrior priests charged up their energy as Zhao-Lan ran up to Corrin.

"What's going on?" he asked, looking Morgana up and down.

Morgana grinned at him, giving him a flirtatious smile.

"Everything is fine. This is Morgana of Aoweii. She's here to help," Corrin said.

Morgana signaled for the other figures to lower their weapons. As they unstrung the arrows, the bows stopped glowing. This intrigued Corrin.

Evrii walked up to Corrin, pushed past Zhao-Lan, and got in Morgana's face.

"I could have killed you," Evrii said sternly.

"I know," Morgana replied, impressed.

"You have a fierce warrior here, Corrin," Morgana said.

Evrii took the compliment and extended her hand. Morgana leaned in and kissed Evrii on the mouth instead.

Corrin and Zhao-Lan froze up.

Morgana pulled away.

"That's how we greet strong women on Aoweii. If you were born Aoweiinian, you would have been a powerful warrior for the goddess Hana."

The other figures took off their face coverings, revealing them all to be women. Morgana walked away. Evrii's cheeks were bright red as she looked over to Corrin who was chuckling.

"Now, let's talk," Morgana said.

The warrior priests chatted with the warriors of Aoweii as Morgana, Corrin, Evrii, and Zhao-Lan sat around a table with wine and bread.

The sun of Arcadia was starting to set and the festivities in the city were beginning to celebrate the end of the summer solstice.

"So, you're all women?" Zhao-Lan cautiously stated.

"Yes, they are, Zhao-Lan," Evrii snapped at him, giving Morgana a friendly smile.

"We're the Order of Hana. Each generation, twelve of us are selected at birth to train and dedicate our lives in the service and protection of Aoweii. It's our most sacred and honorable tradition," Morgana said proudly.

"But it's just twelve of you," Corrin said, concerned they might not be enough and that Emoran exaggerated Aoweii's intent to help.

"Twelve of us who infiltrated Arcadia days ago with ease. We've been on your world watching and learning, studying your movements. None of you had any idea we were here," Morgana replied cockily, taking a sip of her wine.

Evrii was impressed. She looked at Corrin, who also was impressed.

Zhao-Lan wasn't.

"You've been on-world for days and are just now making yourself known?" Zhao-Lan said loudly, then looked at Corrin. "How do we know we can trust her? Them?"

The Order of Hana and the warrior priests all looked over to the table. Silence fell across the room.

"We did this to show you how weak Arcadia's defenses are. We meant no offense. Anti-carrier blasters from Aoweii will arrive at first light to defend Arcadia's atmosphere," Morgana said, putting Zhao-Lan's mind at rest.

Zhao-Lan sat back in his seat, taking a big sip of his wine.

"Thank you," Corrin said, raising his glass.

The others raised theirs as well.

"To new alliances," Evrii proclaimed.

"To new friends," Morgana said.

They all drank.

The next morning the anti-carrier blasters arrived just as Morgana had said. They were massive and outmatched the smaller, less modern weapons Arcadia had.

The Order of Hana showed the warrior priests how to operate them as Aoweiinian technicians made sure they were functioning properly.

Morgana and Corrin walked through the streets of Arcadia. Remnants of last night's festivities were scattered on the streets. Children played and ran up to Corrin, handing him thatch dolls they made of him.

"You've built something remarkable here," Morgana said in awe. "The first planet to host different cultures and people living in harmony together."

"It's why we must defeat my Father," Corrin said solemnly.

Morgana looked at Corrin, trying to read and understand him better. "And are you willing to do what's necessary to stop him?"

Corrin stopped in his tracks, unsure what she meant.

"What do you mean?" he asked.

"If this war is won and we are victorious—will you be able to take the throne from your Father?"

Corrin was agitated by the question. He gave her the same answer he had given Zhao-Lan the day before.

"I do not want the throne. The universe must learn how to rule itself. The worlds are ready for that!"

Morgana took a moment to respond, finally understanding Corrin. "Good. Then let's win this war," she said, walking ahead.

Corrin was shocked to hear her agree with him. He followed her.

As they reached the highest hill in Arcadia, Corrin and Morgana overlooked the city and watched the anti-carrier weapons being put into place along the clouds.

"Why does Aoweii have these weapons? The Black Palace has never bothered you," Corrin asked.

"They weren't made to fight off The Black Palace," Morgana said, her voice breaking a little.

"Who were they made to fight, then?"

"Xarvem," Morgana said quietly.

When The All Father took over the universe again after Helena's death, Aoweii submitted out of fear of how powerful the Spear of Space was. The return of The All Father launched Aoweii into a civil war between two factions, those who wanted to continue Aoweii's tradition of worshipping their goddess Hana, and those who believed The All Father was the one true God. The elves who worshipped The All Father were banished to an abandoned moon near Aoweii to live as a cult-like society that worshipped The All Father. They renamed the moon Xarvem, which means *majesty* in Aoweiinian. Ever since then, they've attacked Aoweii occasionally, claiming the elves who live there are heretics and an abomination that needs to be destroyed.

"I've never heard of this," Corrin said, taken aback.

"Of course not. Aoweii keeps its history and secrets to itself. I doubt The All Father would want it known that there's a moon full of zealots out there," Morgana said, shaking her head. "They killed my brother on their last raid. It ruined my house. My father hasn't been the same since."

Corrin could feel the pain in Morgana's voice. His Father's chaos was ruining lives everywhere.

"Lord Corrin."

Morgana and Corrin turned. A warrior priest approached them. "The emissaries have returned."

Out of the Arcadian clouds, fleets of warships descended. The full Kaasian military arrived with General Dalire leading it. Kaasian war banners flowed in the wind as the fleet reached the ground. More followed.

Flags from Scav, Fargulk, Taelvum, and Vaxlier could be seen. The Order of Hana and the warrior priests gathered as the fleet landed and soldiers began piling out. They were young, old, small, and large. Different races of people and beings coming together to fight alongside Corrin.

Tents and barracks were set up as Corrin and the emissaries spoke about their next move. Differences of opinions were well noted.

"We should unleash a full-scale attack on The Black Palace immediately," General Dalire proposed.

The Kaasian lieutenants and officers Dalire brought with him agreed unanimously. They wanted to invade The Black Palace and dispose of The All Father right away.

"An invasion on The Black Palace would be disastrous," General Scibro yelled, standing up from his seat. He was from Fargulk and massive. His height towered over everyone in the room. The black beard he sported was braided, which took focus away from the battle scars on his face. His chest plate was covered in wool and littered with medals and honors.

"The Kaasians would wish us Fargulkians to lead the charge and deplete our numbers as they watch from safety."

General Dalire scoffed.

"Of course, Fargulk doesn't want to take action that will benefit anyone but themselves."

General Scibro and his Fargulkian men grunted. "Tell him. Tell him, Kaasian. *Tell Corrin how Kaasiar* still uses descendants of Fargulkian slaves to work their fields for little to no pay!"

Scibro pounded his fist on the table.

"You seem to be forgetting, Fargulkian, that it was *your people* who sided with the Itarians and who came to *my* world looking for bounty and conquest. My ancestors fought bravely to defend the valleys of Kaasiar from your hordes."

"Let's settle this here, then," Scibro yelled, standing.

Dalire and his men stood as well, drawing their weapons. The tension in the room was thick.

Corrin sat in silence as his new allies were ready to fight each other.

Morgana stood. "No matter the quarrel our planets have had in the past, our common enemy is The All Father. You men with your petty disagreements have been a shackle toward liberation," Morgana said, rolling her eyes.

The generals scoffed, murmuring amongst themselves. General Dalire and his men sat back down, still gripping their weapons.

"You speak of shackling liberation, but where has Aoweii been?" General Scibro asked, facing Morgana.

All the other generals fell silent.

"With Aoweii's full military and power, we could have risen long ago. It was your father's ancestors who defeated the Itarians in the eighth cycle, but now Aoweii has abandoned the universe. And he sends his daughter to fight for him. Where is the great Kronak?"

Morgana swallowed hard but stood strong and moved for the blade on her side.

Corrin interceded instead. "You all have traveled far and have made your propositions known. An immediate invasion of The Black Palace could work but will ultimately fail. My Father…"

Corrin stopped for a moment.

"*The* All Father has one thing that will cripple our advancements at first sight. The Spear of Space."

A gust of shivers took over the room.

"I was there on Halvodon when he used the Spear to eradicate the remainder of an entire civilization," Corrin said, feeling ashamed at what his Father did. "Our numbers stand no chance against it."

Morgana looked at him with a sense of pity.

"In order for this campaign—this war—to succeed, liberating *all* the planets must come first. Along the way we can amass a force so grand that The All Father will have no choice but to surrender. Once he realizes that the entirety of his kingdom is in open revolt, he *will* step down. Despite The Black Palace being his stronghold, there are still innocent people and families that live on-world. An immediate invasion will put them at risk. And I am not leading a slaughter of those who have not taken up arms against us!"

"What makes you think The All Father will just surrender without a fight?" General Ra-Lin spoke, breaking his silence.

Ra-Lin was of Vaxlier, a world consumed of lava where some of the strongest weapons in the universe were made. His petite stature made him an efficient and quick fighter.

"The All Father won't risk destroying everything he's built. If we give him a false sense of hope that he can maybe one day regain power, he will surrender. And during that gesture, we seize the Spear and imprison him for his crimes!"

The room erupted in cheers. Warrior priests, the Order of Hana, and commanders from the different worlds all were on board with Corrin's plan.

General Dalire had doubt written all over his face but still approved.

General Scibro walked over to Corrin, towering over him. "Let's hope you're not wrong," Scibro said.

CHAPTER 11

THE ALLEGIANCE

The campaign to liberate the planets started with Pugart. It was there that Corrin began to have doubts as an adult about his place within his Father's world. To Corrin, it only seemed appropriate to have Pugart be the first planet he fought for, not against.

The armies under Corrin's command quickly overtook The Black Palace soldiers stationed there.

The people of Pugart were accustomed to constantly being ruled by foreign diplomats appointed by The All Father but now felt a sense of self-determination for being able to finally dictate their own future.

Bloodied from battle, General Scibro approached Corrin, who was ordering captured Black Palace soldiers to be put on trial by a court of Pugarts.

"The main cities have been taken and all The Black Palace diplomats have been arrested. The capital is moments away from being yours. General Dalire, with all his Kaasian pomp, is a master of war."

Corrin was glad to hear of the progress but taken aback by Scibro's statement.

"That's great news, General, but the capital is not mine. It belongs to the people of Pugart." Corrin began walking away.

"Yes, but who will stay in charge to lead this country to a better future? Surely you will appoint a governor that will implement your will," Scibro stated.

Corrin turned back to him. "No one will ever be appointed by me to dictate what others wish for their lives. Never!"

Corrin turned away again, thinking this was the end of the conversation.

"But, Corrin, I have seen what happens when a planet is allowed to decide its own future. When Fargulk revolted against your Father, when you were just a boy, we thought our own leaders would have our best interest in mind, but all that thought did was lead us right back into the hands of The All Father. The same will happen here!"

Corrin didn't turn back to look at him this time. The contempt Scibro had for his decision bothered Corrin. "My decision is final."

Corrin walked away.

General Scibro glared at him.

Later that night, Morgana and Zhao-Lan entered Corrin's tent. Corrin was still thinking about what General Scibro had said.

"News from the capital is that Dalire has rounded up the remaining Black Palace soldiers and is making his way back to us now. We liberated the planet in less than a month," Zhao-Lan proclaimed with pride.

Morgana could tell something was occupying Corrin's mind.

"Do we think The All Father will be sending forces to retake the planet?" Zhao-Lan asked.

Corrin was still silent. After a moment, he turned to them. "Most likely. Yes. What're your thoughts on General Scibro?" Corrin asked.

"Loud. Big. Arrogant but a skilled warrior," Zhao-Lan said.

Corrin sat thinking.

"Why do you ask?" Morgana said, trying to get a feel for what Corrin was thinking.

"I don't want this planet to fall again to The All Father, but I also don't want to be seen as appointing governors or magistrates to act as regents in my absence as if I am Pugart's new ruler. I am not leading this war to replace my Father," Corrin said, his voice getting loud and agitated.

For the first time, Zhao-Lan didn't know what to say. But Morgana understood Corrin's plight.

"You don't have to appoint someone to lead Pugart toward the future, but you can leave them with the tools needed to defend themselves," Morgana said, giving Corrin a sense of reassurance.

"She's right," Zhao-Lan chimed in.

"As we move on to the other worlds, weapon caches can be set up and left behind to protect them from a Black Palace invasion. Progress made must be kept but not at the expense of the reason behind the fight."

The next morning, General Dalire had returned from the capital and was sharing his stories of battle amongst the soldiers and generals. Corrin approached them, eager to hear.

"The Black Palace cowards fled at the sight of our banners. We found one of the diplomats stuffing a bag full of Pugart gold in an attempt to bribe us. The fool was put in chains and delivered to the people of Pugart for his crimes," Dalire boasted.

The men around him cheered. Corrin smiled as Dalire stood and walked up to him.

"Your win will make a great song one day," Corrin said, laughing with Dalire.

"Songs will be written about this war, Corrin. We will win."

"I am planning on leaving weapon caches scattered across all major cities in case The All Father sends a fleet to take the planet. Do you agree with this decision?" Corrin asked, fearing what Dalire would say.

Dalire pondered Corrin's question for a moment before answering.

"Yes," Dalire said, giving Corrin a sense of relief. "We need our forces with us for the next battles that are ahead, but amongst us all we have more than enough weapons and defense to leave behind as we liberate these worlds."

Corrin was relieved to hear Dalire say that. As they exchanged embraces of support, General Ra-Lin approached them.

"We've received word from the southern province of Tenloh that Pugarts are banding together under our banners to protect and fight for their world. They're saying they are now part of 'The Allegiance,'" Ra-Lin said, smirking.

Dalire and Corrin grinned.

"The Allegiance? Has a good ring to it," Dalire said, cheering.

He turned and faced the entire base camp. *"To The Allegiance!"* he yelled.

The entire base camp roared back. Morgana and the Order of Hana lifted up their blades.

"The Allegiance!" they yelled.

The entire base camp chanted *The Allegiance*. Corrin looked at them all with pride. This war was going to shape the universe into one of peace and prosperity.

On The Black Palace, things weren't looking as hopeful.

"You advised me to continue onward to the new worlds because Corrin's forces were defeated!" The All Father yelled at General Kartov, who feared to look into The All Father's eyes.

"Look at me when *I speak* to you," The All Father decreed, rising up from his seat, his white eyes glowing with fury.

General Kartov lifted his eyes, dread pouring out of them. The other generals sat in complete silence.

The All Father descended to his seat. He was breathing hard and heavily.

Dyerian was in the back corner with Grater grinning, while Grater's conscience continued to weigh him down.

"My son is now in open war against me and the fools I appointed as generals have nothing to say for it," The All Father said aloud to himself. Or to the Spear.

"Who are you speaking to, my liege?" General Kartov mumbled.

The All Father took offense to this question and zoomed to Kartov, punching a hole through his chest.

Grater's jaw dropped as the other generals tried their hardest not to let out a sound. Kartov gasped for air as The All Father held his lungs. Dyerian took the opportunity to step forward.

"All Father, Corrin has once again shown you that he will not rest until he has overthrown you. Give me command of your military and I will put an end to his unjust offenses toward you," Dyerian demanded.

The All Father pulled his arm out of Kartov's chest, allowing Kartov's lifeless body to collapse to the floor.

Dyerian stood there amongst all the generals glaring at him for trying to take their power away.

The All Father returned to his seat and sat down, unfazed.

"All Father—" Dyerian began to say again, before being cut off.

"Send out spies to gather intel on what exactly Corrin plans to do. I want to know how large his forces are. His numbers. His cavalry. The size of his fleet. Generals, do not disappoint me again," The All Father solemnly said.

The generals got to work immediately, leaving Dyerian confused and embarrassed. Grater grinned.

As Dyerian began to leave as well, The All Father stopped him.

"Fargulkian, remove this body from my presence."

Dyerian flared his nostrils and did as he was told.

After Pugart was liberated, The Allegiance moved on to LweeVeer. The interconnected planets of Lwee and Veer were already up in arms against Black Palace soldiers. Even the zealots who wanted to destroy the bridge that connected both planets fought alongside The Allegiance.

Weapon caches were left on every liberated planet, allowing the inhabitants of each world to have a fair fight against Black Palace troops. Spacecrafts were left behind in order to stop invading ships. Turret defenses were spread across atmospheres. Every woman, man, and child who was able to fight was given a blaster and energy sword to defend their homes. Air battles, skirmishes in most cities, and revolts were seen across the universe now as Black Palace troops were being stopped in their tracks by people who wanted freedom.

Next, The Allegiance sieged upon the Black Palace military strongholds on the planet Scav. The emissary Sergex prepared the planet's fire warriors and they joined Corrin and The Allegiance. The ancient fire warriors who used spear energy to manipulate the element of fire were formidable and fierce fighters. Together they retook Scav and ousted The Black Palace foreigners who had converted the red planet into a classist society.

On Gorkon, mine workers from the small planet fought bravely and viciously alongside The Allegiance when they arrived.

News of The Allegiance spread like wildfire across the universe. More and more planets were sparking their own rebellions against Black Palace occupying forces.

The Allegiance was becoming a symbol. Banners could be seen waving from liberated cities with The Allegiance's insignia. Battles were spread across the universe of worlds fighting against The All Father in the name of freedom.

But on the planet Kkooddrraa sentiments of war and joining forces with Corrin was not on the minds of the junkyard, criminally controlled world.

"Morgana has sent word that the fire warriors of Scav and the ice warriors of Catovaz will be rendezvousing with her on Itarus to then meet us here," General Ra-Lin said to Corrin, who was overlooking what seemed to be the capital of Kkooddrraa.

"Good," responded Corrin.

"Are you sure about this?" said General Dalire, peering out into the lawless main city of Kkooddrraa.

"We've been on this campaign for months now," said Corrin. "Our numbers are depleted. The wounded are slowly starting to outnumber able-bodied fighters and The All Father has already begun to send forces out to reclaim lost territory."

Corrin was already starting to look worn-out from battle. His beard was long and thick. His hair had grown even longer than before. His eyes were sunken but determined. Zhao-Lan, who had been injured in the Battle for Scav, approached them.

"Ah, the infamous city that makes Kkooddrraa, well, Kkooddrraa," said Zhao-Lan, aching from the injury on his side.

"Zhao-Lan, you should be resting," Corrin said, stepping up to Zhao-Lan to make sure he could stand.

"I'm OK, my lord," Zhao-Lan said, grateful that Corrin was concerned.

"So, who is this Aklan you are meeting?"

"He calls himself 'the Warlord of Warlords,'" Corrin said, peering back into the city.

"If he is what he claims to be, then he's the man to speak to in regards to getting support from Kkooddrraa."

"These are lawless men," General Dalire said.

"It's war," General Scibro said, appearing out of nowhere.

Everyone turned to look at him.

"There's no time to sit on moral ambiguity. Let's meet the son of a bitch," Scibro said, walking ahead.

Dalire, Ra-Lin, and Zhao-Lan all looked at each other, then at Corrin, who let out a sigh of agreement.

They all went toward the city, ready to meet Aklan the Warlord.

Out in the deep reaches of the universe, past the Faoder Sector, The All Father floated in the darkness of space. He held the Spear of Space and thought deeply.

His eyes were closed as if he was mediating or remembering a time before. The silence of space consumed his mind before a small, one-man pod approached. General Nafo-Veguz exited the pod in a Black Palace space suit and floated up to The All Father.

"Our spies have informed us that Corrin's forces are indeed larger than we anticipated. Although your soldiers did deliver a big blow to his numbers on Scav, our intelligence now says he's on Kkooddrraa meeting with an outlaw named Aklan, the Warlord of Warlords, to talk some sort of alliance."

"You've always been loyal to me, Nafo-Veguz. I will remember that," The All Father said, his eyes now staring out into space.

"Send word to all the planets who are aligned with The Black Palace. If my son wants a war, I will give him one."

General Nafo-Veguz bowed his head and returned to his pod. As the pod made its course back to The Black Palace, Nafo-Veguz turned his head to look back at The All Father.

Out of the darkness of space, he watched as The All Father used the Spear of Space to open a small portal. Nafo-Veguz leaned in to get a better look as hundreds, even thousands, of hands and arms began to force their way out of the portal.

Back on Kkooddrraa, the streets of the main city were filled with outlaws from all the planets. Criminals of all sorts created an entire city where everything and anything was considered legal. No one there cared about who lived or died.

Corrin, Dalire, Zhao-Lan, Ra-Lin, and Scibro were stared at. Not because they were seen as a threat but as potential marks for thieves to catch a quick score.

"Should we have come down here severely outnumbered?" Zhao-Lan asked, charging up his energy blasts just in case.

"If they assassinate me here, then I deserve it," Corrin said, laughing.

Up ahead of them stood a massive building made up of broken jet parts, a decommissioned carrier ship from the Itarian era, and other junk. Guards were seated at the front of the door drinking and gambling, while women made their way to Corrin and his commanders.

They admired their armor and battle scars. Scibro was enjoying the praise. Corrin walked up to the door but was stopped by a guard who pushed him back.

"Who the hell are you?" he said, sizing Corrin up. The man was large and almost passed for a Fargulkian. His bald head was littered with tattoos and he was missing an eye. He smelled horribly.

"I'm Corrin—I'm here to see Aklan."

A woman stood up and circled Corrin. She was petite and had two pigtails. She had a large blaster strapped to her waist and was caressing it as she checked Corrin out. Dalire had his blade gripped just in case.

"So, you're *the* Corrin, huh?" she said, seemingly unimpressed. "I thought he'd be taller," she said, making her way back to her seat.

The men around her laughed.

"I'm here to speak with Aklan. I have a proposition for him," Corrin said.

"Aklan doesn't take propositions, pretty boy," a man said.

He was extremely built and his black skin glowed under the Kkooddrraa sun. He was wearing Black Palace armor pants and had shell casings strapped around his tan tank top. His right arm was wrapped in armor, and leaning beside him was a massive axe with a blaster attached to the other end.

"You're a Black Palace soldier?" Corrin asked, pointing to his pants.

"Was," the man said.

"A deserter," Dalire said, spitting on the ground.

"Yeah, what about it? Rather ride out here with these folks than live out my life serving a master I was forced to," the man said, standing up and getting into Dalire's face.

"You were a conscript. Forced by The All Father to join his armies. Probably at a young age," Corrin said, getting in between the man and Dalire.

"That's why I'm here. We are fighting to end everything The All Father stands for."

The other guards began to listen.

Corrin continued, "You've all been outcast and sent here to live out your days as criminals and scum of the universe. You don't have to be the women and men The All Father's diplomats have made you out to be. We can forge a better universe together."

The guards sat in silence for a moment before clapping broke it.

Corrin turned to see an older woman at the doorway. She had long gray hair but her body was firm. She wore a long dark brown cloak and heavy boots meant for the terrain of Gorkon. Her legs were strapped with blades of all sorts and she sported a crown of bones.

"Impressive speech, boy," she said, grabbing a drink away from one of the guard's mouths and slurping it down. "So, you've come to make a proposition to Aklan, the Warlord of Warlords."

"I've come to speak with him, yes," Corrin said, taken aback by this older woman's brazenness.

She let out a laugh.

Everyone except Corrin, Ra-Lin, Dalire, Zhao-Lan, and Scibro got the joke.

"Stupid boy, you desperately need a new understanding of this universe if you think Aklan is a man," she said, waving for Corrin and his comrades to follow her inside.

Corrin looked back at Dalire, Zhao-Lan, Ra-Lin, and Scibro, who were all just as confused as he was.

Inside the hut, the older woman sat down on a makeshift throne. She motioned for Corrin and his commanders to have a seat on the ground. They hesitated but did it anyway.

"So, you've come asking for my help," the older woman said.

"You're Aklan, the Warlord of Warlords?" Scibro said, letting out a laugh.

Corrin clenched his jaw.

Aklan stood up from her seat and approached Scibro, who even seated was taller than her.

"Stand up, Fargulkian," Aklan said, smirking.

As Scibro stood up, he was about four times taller than her.

"Hit me," Aklan said.

Corrin's eyes widened.

Scibro let out a nervous laugh.

"I'm not going to hit an old woman," he said, looking around.

Everyone in the room had no expression on their face. The woman with pigtails was excited to see what was about to happen.

"Do it!" Aklan demanded.

Scibro looked at Corrin, he mouthed *go ahead*.

General Scibro then threw a heavy punch at Aklan, who evaded it and hip-tossed Scibro to the ground, pinning him to the floor with her knee placed on his neck. Corrin had never seen a Fargulkian be tossed around so easily.

She released her leg and went back to her seat. Scibro jumped up immediately and tried to approach her, but the guards in the room drew their weapons.

Corrin stood up immediately. "Scibro, enough," Corrin yelled.

General Scibro was furious but backed off.

Dalire, Ra-Lin, and Zhao-Lan were in shock but impressed.

Corrin turned to face Aklan and made his reasoning for being there very clear.

"You have shown us that you are indeed Aklan, the Warlord of Warlords. I'm asking you to help us defeat The All Father and join our fight," Corrin said, tired of the games.

Aklan sat back down on her throne and ordered a young boy to bring her a drink.

"No," she said, snatching the drink away from the young boy and waving him away.

"Kkooddrraa is fine where we stand. We've never been asked our opinions on universal matters so why should we make alliances with you. You, who for years sided with your Father? And now has found some sort of moral high ground to demand us to fight your battles. Your hands are filled with the blood of the innocent. No war will wash that away."

Corrin didn't know what to say. Aklan was right and he knew it. But he stood his ground anyway.

"You are right. No war, no battles or victories will wash away what I have done in the service of The All Father. I can only atone for my crimes against the people of this universe by ridding it of my Father and ensuring that the planets forge their own path! And you all can help me," Corrin said, looking around.

The mood in the room wasn't in favor until the woman with pigtails stepped forward.

"I'll join you," she said, looking around.

"Yeah, I'm in," the former Black Palace soldier said, his giant makeshift axe hanging from his shoulder.

Corrin and his comrades were delighted. Scibro was still angry from being embarrassed.

Corrin looked at Aklan who rolled her eyes.

"This is Kkooddrraa, everyone here makes their own decisions. If these fools want to join you, I won't stop them. Now get out of my house."

Corrin and his commanders got up and left with the pigtailed woman and the former Black Palace soldier.

Outside they stood around, formally introducing themselves.

"I'm Keelo," the pigtailed woman said. "And this is Reza," she added, pointing at the former Black Palace soldier.

"We know we're not what you were expecting, but we are willing to fight," Reza said, gripping his axe.

"Anyone can make a difference. One or ten thousand is enough," Corrin said.

"We would have *liked* the ten thousand," Dalire said jokingly.

Scibro was far away from them, still trying to heal his ego.

"We have a ship full of weapons and cargo we could add to your inventory," Keelo said excitedly.

"Yeah, it's a few klicks from here. We can go grab it and meet you at your base camp. Try to recruit some people along the way," Reza added.

Corrin agreed and they went their separate ways. On the way back to base camp, Zhao-Lan asked the question that was surely on everyone's minds.

"We all know why Reza is here. He's a deserter. But what the hell did the little pigtailed girl do?"

"I don't want to find out," Dalire said, as they reached base camp.

The Allegiance was set up on the outskirts of Kkooddrraa. As they waited for the return of Reza and Keelo to make way to the next planet, a Kaasian ship entered the atmosphere.

"Dalire, were we expecting reinforcements?" one of the Kaasian lieutenants asked.

The ship was coming in fast. Corrin was concerned and ordered the warrior priests to be on alert.

As the ship landed, a Kaasian soldier exited. He was badly wounded and had a burned handprint on his arm. As he reached Dalire he could barely stand.

"Kaasiar is under attack, General," the soldier said quickly.

"Get this man to medical immediately," one of the Kaasian lieutenants yelled.

The soldier was carried off to a medical tent as Dalire took in the news.

"We have family on Kaasiar, Dalire," another Kaasian lieutenant stated.

Corrin was concerned that Dalire would leave with the Kaasian army, which made up the majority of The Allegiance's forces.

"Corrin," Dalire said, looking at him with regretful eyes.

Corrin knew Dalire had to go save Kaasiar and was ready to join him.

"The Allegiance will fight with you, Dalire", Corrin said with a determined tone.

Morgana and Zhao-Lan nodded their heads in agreement. Ra-Lin stood firm, ready as well.

Dalire looked around as The Allegiance showed that they were willing to take the fight to the green planet. But, Dalire bowed his head.

"I cannot ask you all to come with me" Dalire solemnly said.

Corrin was confused.

"But we are united. We've gotten this far together already, we will not abandon you now!" Corrin said, fazed by Dalire's words.

Dalire lifted his head.

"You are the future of this universe. You are the beacon of hope we've all been waiting for. We cannot risk losing you after so much has been gained."

Corrin listened.

"The people of Kaasiar have fire in their heart. By the time we arrive, who knows, the enemy might already be defeated" Dalire said proudly, letting out a chuckle that slightly masked a hint of fear.

Corrin contemplated on what Dalire was saying, wanting to disagree and go fight with the man who had became somewhat of a brother to him. But he understood.

"Go. We will wait for you here" Corrin said as the sun of Kkooddrraa casted an ominous shadow over the base camp.

Dalire approached him and they locked arms.

"I will eradicate the forces that dared to invade Kaasiar," Dalire said solemnly.

Corrin, Zhao-Lan, Ra-Lin, and General Scibro watched as Dalire and the entire Kaasian fleet took off into space.

As General Dalire and the entire Kaasian army arrived at Kaasiar a day later, they were ready to engage in immediate combat. But the planet's atmosphere had no Black Palace carrier ships waiting for them.

Fires could be seen from space across the entire planet. As the Kaasian fleet descended through the clouds, they weren't met with artillery. The fleet landed without pushback from ground forces.

As General Dalire marched the army to the capital, the city was in ruins. But no sign of a siege or battle had been left behind.

"What happened here?" one of the lieutenants asked chillingly.

Out of the smoke a screech was heard. It was a sound Dalire, his lieutenants, and men had never heard before.

"Men, draw your weapons," Dalire yelled.

The Kaasian army let out a unified roar and pulled out their swords. They waited to be charged at but nothing happened. Dalire could feel a cold sweat trickling down his neck.

"Wait, what...*what is that?*" a soldier from the back line yelled.

As Dalire turned, thousands of creatures leaped from the crumbling buildings onto the soldiers, disintegrating them upon contact. More creatures came pouring out of the smoke, trampling over each other, engulfing the entire Kaasian army.

CHAPTER 12

THE FIRST YEAR

After a month with no word from Kaasiar, Corrin sent out scouts from the base camp on Kkooddrraa to go see what happened. Deep down in his gut, Corrin knew something was wrong. The Allegiance had lost contact with the Kaasian fleet. General Dalire had taken the entire Kaasian army to go defend Kaasiar and his absence left a massive hole, not only in The Allegiance's forces, but in Corrin's hope to win the war.

Morgana had already arrived with new recruits from the worlds of Scav and Catovaz.

The Catovazans were skilled warriors who used spear energy to manipulate the element of ice.

Scribes from Ovaseryn said these individuals were potent with power from the Spears, while others declared them abominations. But regardless, Corrin needed them now more than ever.

"It's been a month, Corrin," Morgana said.

Corrin, Morgana, Zhao-Lan, who was now fully healed, Scibro, and Ra-Lin all sat around a fire. The air on Kkooddrraa was getting colder by the day. Troops were beginning to develop sicknesses as food rations dwindled throughout the camp.

"We need to move on," General Scibro demanded, displeased at the amount of time that had been wasted sitting around for Dalire and the Kaasian army to return.

"Scibro is right, Lord Corrin," Ra-Lin added.

"The troops are starving. My scouts from the worlds we freed are telling me The Black Palace has instituted a no quarter law. Everyone associated with The Allegiance, or who even mutters your name, is being put to death."

Corrin sat patiently.

The news bothered him tremendously, but he couldn't bear to think about leaving, not without knowing if Dalire and his men were alive or not.

As Morgana, Zhao-Lan, Scibro, and Ra-Lin sat waiting to hear what Corrin wanted to do, a warrior priest came running into the tent.

"Lord Corrin," she yelled.

"The scouts have returned!"

Corrin burst out of his seat. The others followed, eager to hear what news the scouts brought.

The scouts were gathered outside. The cruiser they were given had been badly damaged. Corrin's mind raced with the worst thoughts imaginable.

As he and the commanders looked at the cruiser dumbfounded, Zhao-Lan broke the silence.

"What news have you?" Zhao-Lan asked impatiently.

The scouts had fear written all over their faces. All of them looked as if they had seen death itself. Silence took over the camp.

"Damn it, men. Speak!" Zhao-Lan said, raising his voice.

One of the scouts stepped forward carrying a helmet.

"We arrived on Kaasiar a week after Lord Corrin sent us out. Black Palace fleets are scavenging the universe, blocking paths, and taking over all refill stations. We tried abandoning the cruiser, but it would have taken us triple the amount of time to get there without a flyer. What we saw on Kaasiar was…was…"

The scout's voice trailed off. He gripped the helmet tighter and stared at it.

"What did you see?" Corrin said, stepping forward.

The scout looked up at him. His eyes were telling a tale of dread Corrin couldn't even fathom.

"Creatures as black as night. Eyes glowing purple with acid for flesh," the scout said trembling.

He lifted the helmet. "This is all that was left of General Dalire."

He handed the helmet to Corrin, who cautiously and painfully took it. He knew how skilled Dalire was on the battlefield, and witnessed the general fighting throughout the battles to liberate the worlds. He had no idea what man or creature could take Dalire down, let alone leave nothing but his helmet behind.

"What evil is waiting for us out there?" Scibro uttered.

Morgana was in deep thought. She had no idea what kind of monsters the scout was speaking of. More soldiers gathered around to listen.

The scout continued, "Bones were littered across Kaasiar. Remains of the army were barely noticeable. Bodies that once wore armor were disintegrated, my lord. We took off as fast as possible but the creatures followed. We only managed to escape once we passed over the asteroid colonies of Braroclyn. The creatures were too preoccupied with consuming the inhabitants there to continue their pursuit. The screams of the people below echoed out into space."

The scout choked on his words. He couldn't bring himself to continue.

Corrin stood there, holding General Dalire's helmet in complete dismay. Zhao-Lan was in utter shock. The other soldiers began whispering amongst themselves.

"How many?" Ra-Lin asked.

"Thousands. Hundreds of thousands," the scout said quickly.

Ra-Lin and Scibro looked at each other with grave concern.

Later that night, orders were given to begin immediate dismantling of the base camp. It was unsure if The Allegiance was going to continue onward as Corrin and his generals debated amongst themselves.

"You heard the scout, warrior priest. Hundreds of thousands of whatever those creatures are took out an entire army. Dalire is dead. This war is over," General Scibro yelled at Zhao-Lan.

"Where's your courage, Fargulkian? How dare you say this war is over? Dalire died fighting for this cause. And you're just going to abandon everything. You coward!"

Zhao-Lan's words pierced through Scibro's brolic chest.

Scibro lunged at Zhao-Lan, throwing a table in front of him across the room. Zhao-Lan charged up his energy.

Morgana got in between them as Ra-Lin grabbed Scibro in an attempt to calm him down.

"You call me a coward, warrior priest? I'll rip those hands right off your small body!" Scibro yelled.

Ra-Lin was strong for his size but was having trouble holding Scibro back.

Morgana was restraining Zhao-Lan, who still had words to say.

"Even with your massive size, your lack of prudence and will to die for something greater than yourself is larger!" Zhao-Lan said angrily, spitting on the floor.

Morgana looked at Corrin, who was still holding General Dalire's helmet.

"Corrin," she said frantically. "What is our next move?"

Corrin looked up at her. He almost had defeat written on his face. The sight of his generals willing to kill themselves did not faze him.

But he spoke anyway. "It's been almost a year since this war has started," Corrin said quietly.

Everyone looked at him.

"I haven't seen my wife or children since we left Arcadia," Corrin continued. He stood up, still holding Dalire's helmet. He paced around the tent, walking over the damaged table Scibro had thrown. "Let's give the troops time to see their families."

"Scibro," Corrin said, looking at him.

Ra-Lin released Scibro, who was still glaring at Zhao-Lan.

"Take your men back to Fargulk. Let them have time with their loves. Their families," Corrin said.

"But, my lord—" Zhao-Lan started, but he was cut off by Corrin.

"Ra-Lin, take the warriors of Scav and Catovaz with you to Yres. I heard General Gaffen is currently in the midst of intense naval battles against The Black Palace Navy."

"Are we dismantling The Allegiance?" Morgana asked, looking at the men in the room who were confused.

"No," Corrin said reassuring them. "We need answers on what these creatures are. I can't find them here and the troops need a moment of peace before we make them fight any enemy we know nothing about. Dalire is dead," Corrin said, taking a moment. "But our cause lives on. Are you all still with me?"

There was a brief moment of silence.

"Always," Zhao-Lan said.

"The Order of Hana is ready to fight and die," Morgana responded.

"I'll take the warriors of Scav and Catovaz to Yres and we'll help General Gaffen send those Black Palace brutes to the bottom of the Indurclian," Ra-Lin proclaimed.

Scibro was silent.

Corrin looked at him.

"What about you, General Scibro? Do we still have the support of Fargulk?" Corrin asked, looking directly into the general's eyes.

Scibro was still visibly angry over his altercation with Zhao-Lan, but he responded to Corrin anyway.

"Fargulk fights for its survival," Scibro said, storming out of the tent.

"Should I stop him?" Morgana asked, pulling out her blade.

"No," Corrin said. "In time we will see where his loyalties are."

The next morning, the Fargulkian troops took off back to Fargulk on Corrin's orders. Ra-Lin, the troops of Vaxlier, and warriors from Scav and Catovaz departed shortly after to Yres. Only Corrin, the warrior priests, the Order of Hana, and their new friends from Kkooddrraa remained.

"So, is the war over?" asked Keelo, who was sitting on Reza's shoulders.

Corrin was standing near a ledge, looking over the deserted junk valleys of Kkooddrraa.

"No," he said, placing General Dalire's helmet on the edge. "It's far from over."

And he was right. The All Father had gathered all the planets who were completely loyal to him and was holding a banquet for them at The Black Palace.

Leaders from desolate planets such as Di were in awe to be in the presence of The All Father.

Tirus, Evrii's father, was there as well. Rashalon took no side after the war broke out, but Tirus accepted

The All Father's invitation to The Black Palace to ensure the safety of his people and planet.

"My son has taken up arms against me. Planets are now in open rebellion against my divine and just rule. But you all have pledged yourself to me by coming here today. When this war is over, you all will reap from the spoils of my generosity," The All Father said, gripping the Spear of Space.

Tirus was completely uncomfortable. And The All Father could tell.

"Tirus," The All Father said.

Tirus looked at him.

All the other leaders fell silent.

"Rashalon sides with me even though its own daughter, your daughter, is married to my disobedient son?"

Tirus chose his next words wisely. "Rashalon appreciates all that The All Father has done throughout his reign. We understand this war as a disagreement between Father and son. We wish to see a quick and swift victory."

"A victory for who?" a reptilian creature from Di asked.

Di was a swamp-like world full of reptilian creatures. A ruthless planet with a deadly political landscape, Di flourished in times of uncertainty, reaping from the benefits of war-torn worlds.

Other desolate leaders mumbled amongst themselves. Tirus shifted in his seat. He could feel the tension in the room growing thicker.

"Well, answer him," Moira said, entering the room with Dyerian and Grater.

From the corner of his eye, Tirus could see Black Palace guards gripping their weapons tighter. He then looked directly at The All Father.

"A victory for whomever is destined to win," Tirus said, thinking he just sealed his fate.

The All Father took offense to Tirus's answer, but didn't react in the way everyone in the room expected.

"A victory for whoever is destined. Tirus, you are correct," The All Father said chillingly. "Now, my generals are reclaiming lost territory as we speak. I ask all of you to remain loyal as The Black Palace brings order back to the universe. I want any utterance of this Allegiance my son has started to be punishable by death on all planets. Di has already begun rounding up suspected sympathizers of Corrin's cause. I expect Rashalon and all the other planets to do the same!"

Tirus and the other leaders got up to return to their worlds.

As Tirus was about to leave, Moira yelled out to him, "Old man. Make sure your whore daughter doesn't get caught alone outside of Arcadia," she said, smirking to Dyerian.

Tirus clenched his jaw and left, hurrying back to Rashalon.

Back on Arcadia, Corrin had already arrived with Morgana, the Order of Hana, Zhao-Lan and the warrior priests, and their new friends from Kkooddrraa.

Lynn and Kale had grown since Corrin last saw them and were becoming skilled warriors. Evrii had been training them every day while leading Arcadia in Corrin's absence.

Later that night, Corrin and Evrii comforted each other.

"The planet seems at peace," Corrin said, his head on Evrii's lap.

Evrii ran her fingers through Corrin's hair. It was longer and thicker than the last time she had seen him.

"The people of Arcadia know what's at stake," she said.

"So do I." Corrin turned his head to look up at her. "Is this war worth risking what we have here?" he asked.

Evrii could tell he was having second thoughts. She knew that it was too late to stop now.

"Yes" she replied. "What you've started has created a ripple effect across the universe. Nothing will ever be the same now. You must finish this. For your children. For Arcadia. For all the worlds."

She leaned down and kissed him. "For me. For us."

Corrin was once again reassured by Evrii's strength. But he still had those creatures on his mind.

"I'm not sure where I'll find the answers to what was unleashed on Kaasiar," Corrin said solemnly.

"Speak to the Time Keeper, maybe?" Evrii said, thinking maybe Zaman would be able to give Corrin the answers he needed.

"Zaman doesn't get involved in these affairs. He would most likely try to talk me out of this war than anything," Corrin said, sitting up. "What about your father?"

"My father?" Evrii responded, confused.

"What would he know?"

Corrin stood up, thinking about all the times he had spent with Tirus and how well versed he was with the history of the universe.

"Maybe he has read something about these creatures throughout his studies or in one of his books. I need to go to Rashalon!"

Evrii could see how determined Corrin was. She didn't want him to leave right away, but she knew this was more important than their love.

"Go," she said.

Corrin was already halfway out the door but turned back to her. "I love you," he said, before racing to Morgana's room.

The next day, Morgana, Corrin, Reza, Keelo, and three other outcasts from Kkooddrraa traveled to Rashalon in secrecy. Black Palace patrols were all over the universe now. Normal pathways to planets were covered in Black Palace ships, making entry into any world nearly impossible.

"Listen, I'm not sure how things are done the way you're from, but we got this. OK?" a friend of Keelo said.

Morgana and Corrin looked at each other, stunned.

"And who are you?" Morgana asked.

"Tolan Fom," Tolan responded, bowing. "My ship is at your service."

He was short and stubby. He had a metal leg and was missing an eye. Morgana was unimpressed and rolled her eyes.

"This is yours?" Corrin asked, looking around.

"Sure is. Made it myself on beautiful Kkooddrraa. Baby can fly faster than any of those Black Palace fighter-class cruisers."

The ship was very makeshift and loud, but flew steady in space. It's engines looked like they were taken from decommissioned carrier crafts from the Itarian era.

"Let's just get there in one piece" Morgana said, as metal shafts from the ships interior rattled.

"And this is your crew, I'm assuming?' asked Corrin, looking around at Reza, Keelo, and two other individuals on the ship.

"Yeah, we never introduced ourselves," one of the other individuals said.

He turned and extended his reptilian hand to Corrin.

"Name's Cavanomaly, Vano for short."

Corrin shook his hand. "You're from Di."

"Yep," Vano said. "Bastards sent me to Kkooddrraa for killing the inbred bastard who massacred my family. Noble son of a whore was an important man. No offense."

"None taken," Corrin said, smiling.

Morgana was still unimpressed with the company they were now keeping.

"And who are you?" Corrin asked, addressing a person who looked like a child.

"That's Essa. She doesn't speak. We found her digging through trash. No one to take care of her," Reza said.

"She doesn't speak, but she'll cut your throat out," Tolan grunted.

Essa was small with long blue hair. She had gray eyes and scars covering her arms. Her waist was littered with blades and she sported two blasters strapped to her back. Morgana's interest piqued just a little.

"We're approaching a checkpoint," Keelo yelled from the front of the ship.

"Let's kill some Black Palace cockroaches," Tolan cheered, turning on a custom-made tank on his back that connected to what looked like a flamethrower on his arm.

"I appreciate your enthusiasm but this is a covert mission," Corrin said, placing his hand on Tolan's flamethrower arm and lowering it. "I just need some information."

Tolan sighed and turned off the tank strapped to his back. "Where's the fun in that?" he muttered.

As the group reached the checkpoint, Corrin came up with a plan.

Keelo, Reza, Tolan, Vano, and Essa were going to proceed en route and engage with The Black Palace checkpoint, as Corrin and Morgana exited the back of the ship and flew into Rashalon.

Morgana was hesitant at first, but Corrin reassured her that his power would protect her. As Keelo pulled the ship into Rashalon's orbit, Black Palace soldiers approached the craft in their space suits. The ship hovered over the planet's atmosphere as Keelo gripped the thrusters in case things went sideways.

Vano and Reza had their blasters ready, as Corrin and Morgana made their exit. Morgana put on a space suit and lowered the helmet.

"Hold on to me," Corrin said.

Morgana took a deep breath as Corrin zoomed out of the ship and into Rashalon's atmosphere.

One of the Black Palace soldiers briefly noticed a glimpse of light.

"What was that?" the Black Palace soldier asked, gripping his blaster.

Tolan quickly answered.

"Just some gas exhaustion from my old girl" Tolan said, nervously smiling.

Corrin and Morgana landed on the outskirts of the capital and made their way to Tirus. Black Palace guards flooded the streets. The people of Rashalon weren't their normal cheerful selves as the occupation was clearly terrifying the citizens.

"Once we get to Tirus, we'll ask him what he knows and get out of here quickly," Corrin whispered, as they shuffled through the streets.

Rashalon had remained neutral as the war broke out. Small revolts sparked in small parts of the planet, but they were quickly extinguished.

"There's too many of them," Corrin said quietly to Morgana as they hid and tried to conceal themselves.

Morgana thought quietly, as she analyzed the situation.

"Is that the building we need to get to?" she asked Corrin, pointing toward the viceroy building far ahead.

"Yes," Corrin responded.

"Follow me," Morgana said.

Corrin followed Morgana's lead as she secretly and cautiously hurried through some alleyways. They climbed up pillars and walls that led them to the rooftops of Rasho homes and stores. Morgana leaped from building to building, landing softly without making noise. Corrin followed her, impressed at just how resourceful and skilled this Aoweiinian was.

As they got closer to the viceroy building, The Black Palace guard presence was larger.

"Wait here," Morgana said.

"Where are you going?" Corrin responded as Morgana disappeared around a corner.

Grunts, body blows, and gasping could be heard. There was silence for a moment after, making Corrin charge up his energy before Morgana came back with Black Palace armor.

"Put this on," she said.

Corrin stared at her.

"Don't just look at me, do it," she said, annoyed.

Corrin put on the armor. It was a little too small for him, but it didn't matter.

"There's too many of them for us to slip through," Morgana said, staring ahead at the countless Black Palace soldiers patrolling the streets. "Never mind, we're going to have to fight our way through." She eagerly pulled out her blades and thrusted forward to engage.

Corrin quickly removed The Black Palace helmet and stopped her.

"Like you said, there's too many of them," Corrin quickly said.

He thought as Morgana put her blades away. Corrin turned back to her, excitement on his face.

"There's a passageway under the building," he quickly and quietly said.

"Evrii showed it to me years ago. Ancient leaders built it during the Itarian era for whenever the city was under siege! It leads right into the viceroy's private quarters."

Morgana rolled her eyes.

"You're just now remembering this?" she said, motioning for Corrin to lead the way. He took off The Black Palace armor and led Morgana to the passageway.

As they reached the tunnel to the passageway, Black Palace troops were approaching. Morgana and Corrin quickly entered before being spotted. They ran down the long corridor that stretched for miles under the city. Low lit torches illuminated the path and showed ancient paintings of the Itarian emperors' cosmic dragons.

"We're here," Corrin said, pushing a wall that opened into a study.

Morgana noticed the wall was the backside of a bookcase. As they entered the room, Corrin quickly hurried to the door, as Black Palace soldiers walked by. As they continued their patrol, Corrin cautiously closed it. Morgana was on edge but kept her composure.

"So, this Tirus, he is the father of Evrii?" Morgana asked, peering out a window that over looked the city.

"Yes," Corrin replied, looking at the books scattered across Tirus's desk. He picked one up. It was the book he and Tirus had both read.

"He's a great man. A father anyone could wish for."

A door that led to a different room opened and a man entered. Morgana quickly pulled out her blades as Corrin charged up his energy before he realized it was Tirus.

"Tirus," Corrin said happily, the energy around his hands dissolving.

"Corrin?" Tirus said with confusion and happiness. He shut the door behind him as Corrin embraced him.

"You look well," Corrin said, checking him out.

Tirus noticed Corrin's disheveled beard and untamed hair.

"You look…you look tired," Tirus said, concerned as to why Corrin was in Rashalon. "Why are you here?"

Corrin and Tirus walked over to chairs and sat down. The same chairs they had their first conversation in over twelve years ago.

Morgana still had her blades out and was peering out the window, making sure there wasn't any sudden commotion or call to soldiers outside.

"I believe my Father has unleashed some sort of creatures to aid him in this war," Corrin said, hoping to hear Tirus respond with knowledge of what they were.

Tirus looked at Morgana.

"Forgive me, this is—"

"Morgana, daughter of Kronak. Leader of the Order of Hana," Tirus answered, standing up to face Morgana.

He bowed to her. "Welcome to Rashalon."

Morgana was impressed that he knew who she was.

"How do you know who I am?" she asked, still cautious of any soldiers that might appear.

"I am friends with your father," Tirus said. "We both share the belief that the universe should be free from The All Father's tyranny."

"So, Rashalon sides with The Allegiance, then," Corrin stated.

"In private," Tirus responded. He walked over to the door, making sure it was locked. "There are those on

Rashalon who wish to stay in the 'good graces' of The All Father."

"Jahgros," Corrin said to himself.

"In regards to what you speak of, I am of no help. We heard reports of creatures devouring planets. Misshapen monstrosities never before seen. I tore through my library, hoping to find something, but whatever The All Father has awoken is not in recorded history." Tirus said chillingly.

Corrin stood up. He didn't know where else to go.

"How is my daughter? The children?" Tirus asked.

Corrin felt like an idiot for not bringing up Evrii, Kale, and Lynn.

"They are great. Kale and Lynn are growing fast. Evrii is everything you raised her to be," Corrin said to Tirus, trying to reassure him that they were safe.

Tirus took ease at hearing Corrin's words.

"This war must end with you victorious. I fear what will happen if you fail," Tirus solemnly said to Corrin.

"If we don't have answers here, where else can we find them?" Morgana asked.

"Ovaseryn," Tirus quickly said, heading to his bookcase.

He ran his finger through the countless books he had before pulling one out.

"You've studied and trained on Ovaseryn, Corrin. If these creatures were unleashed by your Father, and if the reports are true of them being entities of immense energy, then the scribes of Ovaseryn will surely have the answers you seek."

Corrin grabbed Tirus and gave him a massive hug.

"Thank you," he said.

Tirus embraced him some more.

"Be safe, Corrin. You're not the Shepherd of Fire anymore. You're the Shepherd of Men now. Your fight will define the future for all of us."

Tirus's words sank deep into Corrin's mind and heart as he and Morgana reentered the passageway and made their way back to Keelo and the others.

As they ran through the passageway, Jahgros hid behind one of the corners, watching as Tirus closed the bookcase wall.

When Corrin and Morgana returned safely to the ship, Reza was pacing back and forth, concern on his face.

"What is it, Reza?" Corrin asked.

"Those creatures that took out your army on Kaasiar have reached Kkooddrraa," Reza said, pointing to Keelo.

"We received a distress beacon from Aklan," Keelo said, replaying an audio recording.

Morgana and Corrin listened in horror as Keelo pressed play.

"If anyone can hear this," Aklan's voice was heard saying on the audio. Screeching and people screaming could also be heard. "Kkooddrraa is under attack. If you're out there, Corrin, please. We need help," Aklan screamed before the audio cut off.

Tolan, Vano, Reza, and the others stood in complete shock after listening to the audio.

Corrin stared at the audio player as his eyebrows burrowed into anger.

"Take us to Kkooddrraa now," he said.

On the way to Kkooddrraa, Morgana used the ship's radio to send word to Ra-Lin, Zhao-Lan, and Scibro to meet them there. When Corrin and the group arrived, the others were waiting for them. The Order of Hana gave Morgana her armor inside their ship as the warrior priests lined up above the planet's atmosphere.

Ra-Lin was ready with the troops from Vaxlier and the fire and ice warriors of Scav and Catovaz.

"Where is General Scibro?" Corrin asked, looking around.

"He did not come," Ra-Lin answered, clenching his jaw.

"And Yres?"

"General Gaffen and kingdoms of Yres sent The Black Palace navy to the bottoms of the oceans," Ra-Lin said proudly.

"Good," Corrin said, turning to face Kkooddrraa.

Reza, Keelo, Tolan, Vano, and Essa were geared up and ready. The Allegiance flew into Kkooddrraa's atmosphere, piercing through the clouds.

Corrin and the warrior priests led the advancements as the rest followed closely behind on a carrier ship.

As they closed in on the ground, the creatures that had destroyed Kaasiar were already flying at them. Warrior priests, the troops from Vaxlier, the fire and ice warriors, and the Order of Hana were getting picked off and devoured by the creatures. The carrier ship they were on was swarmed by the creatures as Corrin watched in horror mid flight as his numbers shrank quickly.

Zhao-Lan was using energy blades to cut through them as Morgana picked them off. She stood on the carrier ship taking on as many as she could.

As they reached the ground, The Allegiance was surrounded by the creatures.

"What are these beings?" Zhao-Lan yelled as dozens of the creatures rushed him.

He evaded them and ripped through their bodies, their entire anatomies dispersing into the air.

Ra-Lin leaped off the carrier and rushed to a soldier of Vaxlier who was wounded. He watched in horror as the creatures disintegrated him upon touching his skin.

As Ra-Lin was struck with shock, the creatures rushed at him before Tolan blew them away with his flamethrower. Essa leaped over Tolan and sliced through their heads to finish them off.

"Watch your back, old man," Tolan said laughing, as he attacked more of the creatures.

The creatures kept coming. Thousands of them leaping and tumbling over each other. The carrier ship was being ripped apart as warrior priests and the Order of Hana tried to fight them off.

"There's too many of them!" Morgana yelled, as she leaped off the carrier ship before it exploded and was engulfed in flames.

The screams of warrior priests and the Order of Hana could be heard as some of them caught ablaze. Reza swung his axe through the creatures, tearing them apart. Corrin used his energy to launch the creatures back, but there were too many of them. Warrior priests were overwhelmed by hundreds of them. It was fifty to one at this point.

"Retreat!" Corrin yelled.

Keelo was hovering above the ground with Tolans ship and descended rapidly. The remaining Order of Hana, Morgana, Ra-Lin, and the rest of the troops piled in as Corrin and the warrior priests charged up their energy to blast into space.

The warriors of Scav and Catovaz were using their ice and fire abilities to kill off the creatures.

"We'll hold them back for as long as we can," a young female warrior from Scav yelled.

Corrin watched in awe as the fire and ice warriors used their individual elemental powers to hold back the creatures.

"For the Allegiance!" an ice warrior of Catovaz yelled as he and his brethren charged towards the creatures.

Corrin and the warrior priests blasted into space as the creatures consumed Kkooddrraa.

From the outer atmosphere, their screeches could be heard from below. Corrin and Morgana both watched as Kkooddrraa was lost to whatever The All Father had released.

Morgana's space suit was badly ruined as she exited Tolan's ship and watched in horror as Kkooddrraa was lost.

"We must go on to Ovaseryn," Corrin said with determination.

The Order of Hana, what remained of them, were badly wounded. Morgana closed her eyes and thought, before turning to Corrin.

"I'm going back to Aoweii," Morgana said.

Corrin looked at her in shock.

"Whatever these creatures are, they could go for Aoweii next. I need to go and prepare for a possible invasion!"

She couldn't look Corrin in the eyes. She felt like she was betraying him. But Corrin understood.

"I understand," he said.

He floated into the darkness of space, so the remaining forces could see and hear him.

"I don't know what we just faced. These creatures, those monsters, are going to come for all of us. Our homes. I will go to Ovaseryn alone to get the answers we need. When I know what we are fighting, then we will be able to defeat them."

The morale amongst what was left of The Allegiance was low.

Ra-Lin had exhaustion and fear written all over his face. Keelo was consoling Essa as Reza, Tolan, and Vano stared at the destruction of their home. Zhao-Lan approached Corrin.

"I'll take the wounded back to Arcadia. Find out how we can destroy these beasts," he said to Corrin.

They embraced before Zhao-Lan left on Tolan's ship.

The Order of Hana waited for Morgana on their Aoweiinian ship as she floated next to Corrin.

"This isn't goodbye," she said through her space suit, trying to make herself believe what she was saying.

"I know," Corrin said, giving her a broken smile.

As she motioned toward the ship, she turned back quickly and embraced Corrin, giving him a reassuring hug. She grabbed his shoulders and looked directly into his eyes. "Get the answers we need!"

She released him, headed to her ship, and took off into the emptiness of the universe.

Corrin watched as the Aoweiinian ship disappeared. Below him Kkooddrraa was completely decimated by the creatures his Father had unleashed.

He was alone in the vast emptiness of space. At any moment the creatures were going to move on to the next planet and continue their devastation.

It had been a full year now since Corrin broke from his Father. A year of war, death, sacrifices, and pain. Lives lost for a better future. Homes burned to the ground in the name of freedom.

The All Father wanted a son to lead the universe. And Corrin was finally starting to understand that he was born to lead. Not to lead the worlds under an iron fist like his Father but toward a future of self-determination.

It had been a full year of war and his armor was covered in dirt and blood. The seal of The All Father was still on Corrin's chest plate.

Corrin hadn't even thought of removing it until now.

He placed his hand on his chest and ripped the seal off. Looking at it brought back all the memories of conquest and death he committed for his Father's approval.

As he took one last look at the seal, he released it and watched it get sucked into Kkooddrraa's orbit and fall into the planet. Corrin was now fully free of The All Father. He took a deep breath and zoomed to Ovaseryn to find the answers he needed.

GLOSSARY

CHARACTERS

Aklan- Lives on Kkooddrraa (pronounced Ca-cu-dra). Aklan is the de-facto leader of the outlaw planet. She is called the warlord of warlords due to her vicious and swift actions. She came to Kkooddrraa as a young girl and quickly rose to power.

Corrin- Son of Helena, Son of The All Father, heir to the universe. Corrin grew up under the iron fist of his father, forged out of fire and war to lead and control the universe when the time came.

Dalire- (pronounced Da-leer) General Dalire, leader of the armed forces of Kaasiar. Alive during the reign of the last Itarian emperor, and witnessed The All Father retake the universe with brute force, Dalire dedicated his life to rebuild the Kaasian army for when the time came to fight for liberation.

Drisa-Yun- Warrior priest from the planet Wan-Ri and one of Corrin's loyalists.

Dyerian- (pronounced Dee-ree-an) Commander within the Black Palace military and long time enemy of Corrin. Dyerian was born on Fargulk and was conscripted into The All Father's forces at a young age.

Emoran- (pronounced Eh-mo-rahn) Emissary from Aoweii and close friend and advisor to Morgana.

Essa- A child with an unknown history. Essa doesn't speak and takes refuge with Keelo and Reza on Kkooddrraa.

Evrii- (pronounced Eh-vree) Born on Rashalon, Evrii was commander of the planet's security forces and loyal daughter to Viceroy Tirus.

Gaffen- General Gaffen leads the naval forces of Yres. Her mastery of the seas became a paramount threat to the Black Palaces naval fleet on her occupied world.

Grater- Grater is Corrin's best friend and grew up in The Black Palace.

Havrene- (pronounced Ha-vreen) A survivor of the Massacre of Halvodon, Havrene was a leader of what remained of the Halvodi civilization.

Havroy- A survivor of the Massacre of Halvodon, Harvoy was a leader of what remained of the Halvodi civilization.

Helena- A daughter of Yres, Helena was the mother of Corrin and wife to The All Father.

Hirvric- (pronounced Her-vric) A survivor of the Massacre of Halvodon. Hirvric was a leader of what remained of the Halvodi civilization.

Hivli- A survivor of the Massacre of Halvodon and son to Havroy.

Horvrin- A survivor of the Massacre of Halvodon, Horvrin was a leader of what remained of the Halvodi civilization.

Jahgros- Functionary Jahgros hails from Rashalon and is a member of one of Rashalon's oldest houses.

Kale- The oldest child of Evrii and Corrin.

Kan- Warrior priest from the planet Wan-Ri and one of Corrin's loyalists.

Keelo- An outlaw from Kkooddrraa.

Lynn- The youngest child of Evrii and Corrin.

Moira- (pronounced Mor-e-ah) Born in The Black Palace to a military family.

Morgana- Descending from Aoweii, Morgana is the leader of The Order of Hana and considered the most skilled and deadliest warrior across the stars.

Nafo-Veguz- Overseeing General of the Black Palace Fleet, Nafo-Veguz served under two Itarian emperors before aligning with The All Father.

Nox/The All Father- Yielder of the Spear of Space and called the creator of life across the universe. Nox, now known as The All Father, is father to Corrin and ruler of all the worlds.

Ra-Lin- General Ra-Lin leads the small armed forces of Vaxlier.

Reza- Reza is a deserter from the Black Palace military. He fled to Kkooddrraa for refuge where he met Keelo, Vano, Tolan, and Essa.

Scibro- (pronounced Ske-bro) General Scibro leads the armed forces of Fargulk. Once a soldier in the Black Palace military, Scibro left to form a secret faction on Fargulk to eventually fight back.

Sun-Tro- Warrior priest from the planet Wan-Ri and one of Corrin's loyalists.

Syeron- (pronounced Sy-ron) From Fargulk and a trusted servant of The All Father, Syeron was Corrin's guardian during his younger years and travels.

Tirus- Father to Evrii and Viceroy of Rashalon, Tirus was elected to be his planet's voice abroad and domestically.

Tolan- Unsure of his origins, but most likely from Vaxlier due to his smaller figure, Tolan is an outlaw living on Kkooddrraa.

Vano- Mercenary and assassin from the planet Di, Cavanomaly, Vano for short, is an outlaw living on Kkooddrraa.

Wi-Lao- Warrior priest from the planet Wan-Ri and one of Corrin's loyalists.

Zaman- (pronounced Zuh-mahn) Yielder of the Spear of Time, Zaman is the keeper of time and all history. He lives alone in the Sanctuary of Time and does not intervene in wars, events, or the natural flow of the universe.

Zhao-Lan- Warrior priest from the planet Wan-Ri, Zhao-Lan is Corrin's most trusted advisor and friend.

PLANETS, PLACES

Aoweii- (pronounced Ah-way)The birth place of Morgana, Aoweii is the planet where the elves of the universe live. Worshipping the goddess Hana, the Aoweiian's train young girls to grow into the fiercest warriors the universe has ever seen. These highly trained women become known as The Order of Hana. Being well tested in battle due to the era of the Itarian empire, Aoweiis army became legendary. When The All Father retook the universe again by force, Aoweii submitted out fear of the Spear of Space, making the worlds lose respect for the once mighty planet. The planet is a mix of large oceans and thick forests, bearing creatures the elves of Aoweii have used for travel, harvesting, and war.

Arcadia- After the death of Helena, The All Father used the Spear of Space to create a planet that would never be destroyed by outside forces. Being able to even withstand the power of the spears, Arcadia was The All Father's creation for Corrin. A utopia of peace, Arcadia became the first planet to harbor people of all worlds when Corrin became Lord. A metropolitan planet and beacon of unity, Arcadia was the stronghold for The Allegiance during the War of the Universe and a place of refugee for those seeking amnesty and safety from war torn worlds.

The Black Palace- Home of The All Father, the Black Palace was the first world created by the Spear of Space. Its main fortress is interconnected with the planet and erects into outer space, giving The All Father a full view of his universal empire.

Braroclyn- (pronounced Bur-ra-co-lin) Named after an Itarian emperor's dragon.
Consisting of colonies of beings who live on asteroids surrounding the planet Jargun-Ba, the colony system known as Braroclyn came to be when one of Jargun-Ba's moons exploded and crash landed on the planet. Before the Itarians began their expansion, the ancient beings of Jargun-Ba were stuck on their moon-wrecked world. When the Itarians came, they helped the inhabitants of Jargun-Ba resettle on the asteroids. Although most inhabitants of Jargun-Ba fled to the asteroid colonies of Braroclyn, those who stayed on Jargun-Ba became plagued with disease and dangerous fumes that filled the air after the devastating moon event. Falling into savagery, the remaining inhabitants of Jargun-Ba feast on the inhabitants of Braroclyn whenever a colony is sucked into Jargun-Ba's orbit and crash lands on its surface.

Catovaz- The ice world known as Catovaz became well known across the universe after they were one of the first planets to fight back against the Itarian empire. With limited sunlight, mountains of snow, and oceans frozen over, the Catovazans were luckily well adapted to their environment and took back their planet from the invaders. Before The Long Sleep, The All Father noticed that spear energy was prevalent in some Catovazans, with certain individuals being able to manipulate the ice and control it at will.

Di- (pronounced Dee)
Called the swamp of the universe due to its muddy landscapes, vicious terrains, and humid air, the gloomy planet known as Di is home to intelligent reptilians who have made their world into a classist society. Loyal to The All Father before and after the war broke out, the reptilian overlords have managed to slither their way into planetary politics as a powerful force.

Eqoulis- (pronounced Eh-kwo-lis)
The sun never sets on Eqoulis. A dangerous planet because people who travel there can easily lose track of time, and eventually lose their minds, Eqoulis is designated as a dead planet. The second largest planet after Fargulk, Eqoulis is littered with large deserts, separating two small patches of civilizations from one another. Journeying to Eqoulis without knowing the

terrain, or where the two small patches of civilization are, is a considered a death sentence across the universe. With massive sand storms happening every hour, crossing the planet's graveyard deserts is almost impossible. Being massive and seemingly uninhabitable, scattered across the planet are remnants and ruins of civilizations that might have been around cycles ago.

Fargulk- Able to fit every planet inside itself, Fargulk is the largest world in the universe. In the early cycles of the universe, giants roamed Fargulk. The giants of Fargulk consisted of people, to water and land creatures, to winged beasts and even plant life. As time went by, the inhabitants of Fargulk, along with all other life, began to shrink in size, but still towered over any other person across the universe. After The Long Sleep, The All Father used the large beings of Fargulk as the first conscripts of his army to retake the planets. Being the largest planet across the universe, most of Fargulk has never been explored and it is said that the true giants still live in the uncharted parts.

Gorkon- Located near The Black Palace, Gorkon is the smallest planet in the universe. A mining world used for its rich minerals, the people of Gorkon live, work, and die underground in servitude to The All Father.

Halvodon- Once a thriving planet with an advanced civilization, Halvodon was a prosperous world. Leaning towards community strength over structures of power, Halvodon was seen as the first planet to put the needs of its people over politics. After The Long Sleep and The All Father's return, Halvodon fought back against joining the empire, and consequently, the flourishing planet was turned into a barren wasteland by the Spear of Space.

Itarus- (pronounced Eh-ta-rus) Itarus was home planet to the once mighty Itarian empire. The Itarians were the first beings to discover space travel during The Long Sleep, and in the fifth cycle they took to the stars, conquering every planet in their path. Laying waste to those who opposed them, the Itarians were invincible as they ravaged the worlds on their cosmic dragons. Towards the end of the eighth cycle, the clans of elves on Aoweii united, and put an end to the Itarian's rule. At the start of the ninth cycle, the Itarians faded into distant memory. Remnants of their once mighty planetary empire can still be seen on most planets. The Itarians left behind landmarks, lifestyles, dialects, accents, culture, and statues that depict the glory, and terror, of their reign.

Jargun-Ba- (pronounced Jah-goon-bah) Destroyed by a moon in the fourth cycle, Jargun-Ba became a barren wasteland. The Itarians helped most of the survivors flee the planet's surface and relocate on the asteroid belt above which would later become known as the colonies of Braroclyn.

Kaasiar- (pronounced Cass-ee-ar) The greenest planet in the universe, and home planet to General Dalire, Kaasiar was the first world to side with Corrin and form The Allegiance. Its history was that of peace and advancement, only becoming militarized when the Itarians invaded. After the return of The All Father, the Kaasian military was presumed disbanded as men and women were forced to be conscripts for The Black Palace. In secret, the full power of Kaasiar was kept underground in preparation for the day they would have to fight for liberation once again.

Kkooddrraa- (pronounced Ca-cu-dra) Kkooddrraa is an outlaw planet with no structural government, leadership, laws, or rules. Used as a junkyard planet for most worlds, Kkooddrraa also became a death sentence for the outlaws and criminals of other planets.

LweeVeer- Two planets make up LweeVeer. They are connected by a bridge that exits the planets and connects them. One planet is called Lwee while the other is called Veer. The space bridge keeps the planets alive by simultaneously feeding off each other's cores. If the bridge was ever broken, the planets would die, killing billions. Inhabitants from Lwee and Veer cross the bridge and travel into each planet whenever they please, but zealots on Veer have tried to destroy the bridge on several occasions.

Myero- (pronounced Mii-row) A highly advanced tech planet seemingly at peace within itself. During the height of the Itarian empire, the brightest minds from Myero were in charge of forging the new technical advancements for the Itarian military. Advanced spacecrafts, weapons, and defense systems were made on Myero. After the fall of the Itarian empire, The All Father continued to use Myeros minds to further the advancement in Black Palace might. The inhabitants of Myero themselves are non-believers in "Gods", spear energy, and abilities. They use science to explain everything.

Nyla- (pronounced Nigh-luh) A massive dark world of rock and ocean. When the Itarians began their expansion, the inhabitants of Nyla moved deep into the planet's caverns, making the Itarians believe the world was too harsh and un-inhabitable. Over the cycles, the Nylans adapted to their way of life hidden under the rocky world, and remained out of sight when The All Father emerged. A civilization comprised of both highly advanced tech, and individuals with strong spear energy, the Nylans decided to keep to themselves hidden away rather than join any war or rebellion.

Ovaseryn- (pronounced Oh-vass-er-rin) The only planet where every inhabitant has spear energy flowing through them, Ovaseryn was the planet where Corrin was sent as a boy to learn how to channel the energy within him. Always at war with two factions, one side believing spear energy makes them superior, while the other side believes spear energy should be used for good, the planet has never been conquered or taken sides with outside quarrels. It is also the only planet Zaman has ever visited.

Pugart- (pronounced Pew-gart) A wealthy dry, desert planet where the elites have subsided most of the planet's resources for themselves. After the fall of the Itarian empire, Pugart's indigenous inhabitants took power and turned the planet into a classist society, in conjecture with the Black Palace.

Qibbi- (pronounced Kwih-bee) Considered a "weird" planet in the universe. The inhabitants never built places of shelter or any aspect of a functioning civilization. Clothes were never made on Qibbi as well as systems of governing, materials for food, or even accessible areas for water. Inhabitants of other worlds usually come to Qibbi for leisure and to relax. When

The All Father retook the universe, he didn't even have to make the inhabitants submit because of the docile state they are constantly in. It was discovered that something from the planet's core gave off a toxic fume that ignites a sense of euphoria and pleasure in the brain.

Rashalon- Taken from a rural planet to a modern, and respectable world by one of Rashalon's oldest houses, this planet became an ally to the Itarians, and later to The All Father. Mostly just for survival, but also so the ruling families can reap the benefits, Rashalon grew in prosperity. Home planet to Evrii, and now under the leadership of Viceroy Tirus, in accordance with The Black Palace, Rashalon has never seen war or anguish.

The Sanctuary of Time- Far out in the universe and almost impossible to travel to without being well trained with spear energy, the Sanctuary of Time is where Zaman dwells. It is where Zaman keeps all records of the universe and the Book of Time.

Scav- A planet covered by cities stacked on each other, the planet Scav has always been a classist society due to its sun. The higher class live on the lower levels of the cities away from the scorching sun, while the middle and lower classes live on the upper levels. The sun is so hot that it burns the skin immediately, so the wealthy live as far away from it as possible. Beings here can manipulate the heat from the sun. In the early cycles, beings on Scav who had spear energy flowing through them were sent to walk the surface of the planet to an ancient pillar, where they would either burn up and die, or manipulate the heat and become fire warriors. The Itarians were never able to conquer this planet but managed to capture some of its fire warriors and use them as soldiers for the Itarian military.

Taelvum- (pronounced Tale-voom) Toxic planet with an un-inhabitable surface. However, the inhabitants were able to build cities on the planet's floating rocks that interact with the planet's core and minimum gravity. Some creatures, and even people, have been rumored to have been able to settle and survive on the planet's surface, but nothing has ever been confirmed. There is also a mysterious race that lives in Taelvum's clouds. Some speculate they have roots tying close to the spears and are named "Sky People".

Telamor- (pronounced Teh-luh-more) Scattered clans of half creature, half people make up Telamor. They were once a united kingdom before a power grab between sisters split the kingdom into clans. When the Itarians invaded, the multiple clans were forced to merge into two, so the Itarians could control them easier. After the fall of the Itarian empire, The All Father took Telamor at ease. It is a mountainous world with barely any leveled ground. The current inhabitants of Telamor believe the universe was better under the Itarians and side with Corrin during the war.

Vaxlier- (pronounced Vax-leer) Lava planet with one landmass. The fountains of Vaxlier are pillars of ancient blacksmiths standing tall with their stone-craft legs deep into the planet's core, allowing the hottest lava to pour through the statues. Some of the strongest hand held weapons in the universe are forged here. It is also the home world of General Ra-Lin. During the Itarian reign, Vaxlierians were trained to be a small terror unit within the Itarian military. After the fall of the Itarian empire, The All Father disbanded them and had the planet's inhabitants return to being stone masons and blacksmiths. Ra-Lin was chosen by his people to lead them to freedom and Vaxlier joined The Allegiance.

Wan-Ri- A world like Ovaseryn where spear energy is revered and respected, Wan-Ri is home to the warrior priests. Unlike the scribes of Ovaseryn who have never left their home planet, the people of Wan-Ri believe it's their duty to help those across the universe and help individuals with spear energy flowing through them to reach their full potential.

Xarvem- (pronounced Zar-vehm) A moon of Aoweii now considered the home world to a cult-like society completely loyal to The All Father. Towards the end of the Itarian empire when whispers began to spread across the universe of the "return of the creator", many elves on Aoweii turned away from worshipping their Goddess Hana and began to worship The All Father as the one true God. Aoweii's Chief banished these zealots and they settled on a moon called Xarvem, where they dedicated their lives to eradicating Aoweii and making it a satellite state for The Black Palace.

Yres- (pronounced Eee-rez) Home world of Corrin's mother, Helena, Yres is a water planet consumed with large oceans. Over ninety five percent of the planet is covered in water. There are five different kingdoms on Yres, two of them consisting of land people, and the other three consisting of under-water beings. They all live in harmony together but have their quarrels here and there. When the Itarians invaded, the five kingdoms of Yres were left to continue their way of life, as did The All Father due to Yres being the home of his lover. Something about Yres being a captivating world of water, and its inhabitants blessed with immense physical beauty, made invaders and would-be conquerors leave the planet untouched.

ITEMS, CREATURES, GROUPS, ABILITIES

The Allegiance- A union amongst certain planets throughout the universe that sided with Corrin in the war against The All Father.

Balakar- (pronounced Bah-lah-car) Native creature from the planet Halvodon. A two legged, bulky, yet quick and sturdy beast, the Balakar was used by Halvodis as a means of travel. After the return of The All Father, Balakars began to be used as a means of war and defense against Black Palace troops.

Cycle- Time frame in the universe. 100,000 years equals one cycle.

Fire Warriors- Legendary warriors from the planet Scav. Individuals with enough spear energy flowing through them are able to manipulate the element of fire.

Functionary- Government position.

THE OLD UNIVERSE

Itarians- The first race to travel the stars. They created intergalactic travel and the first planetary empire.

Ice Warriors- Legendary warriors from the planet Catovaz. Individuals with enough spear energy flowing through them are able to manipulate the element of water and covert it into ice.

Order of Hana- Group of elite warriors and assassins from the planet Aoweii. The Order consists of twelve women chosen at birth to be the planet's most skilled and deadliest defenders.

The Scribes of Ovaseryn- Beings from the planet Ovaseryn who are well versed and well trained with the cosmic arts and spear energy. The scribes were amongst the oldest beings in the universe and the only beings, other than The All Father and Corrin, who have met, spoken with, and studied with Zaman.

Spear Energy- Power flowing through individuals. When The All Father used the Spear of Space to create life, energy from the Spear of Space was so pure it transcended into certain life forms, giving them the ability to use the power.

The Spear of Space- Held by The All Father, the Spear of Space created the universe after clashing with the Spear of Time.

The Spear of Time- Held by Zaman, the Spear of Time created the universe after clashing with the Spear of Space.

Vasari- (pronounced Vuh-sar-ree) Revered four legged creature on the planet Rashalon, Vasaris are seen as more than just animals by the Rasho people. Dating back to Rashalon's earliest civilization, Vasaris became a symbol of Rashalon's pride of starting off as nomadic tribesmen, to one of the most respected planets in the universe.

Viceroy- Government position.

Warrior Priests- Warriors from Wa-Rin who have trained from birth to master the spear energy flowing inside them.

Made in the USA
Monee, IL
06 April 2024